KAKORI

Praise for the author and her works

"...priceless tips for startup expansion and management. *[Ganesha's Global Startup]* is a must read..."

– *The Times of India*

"...handpicked success mantras... *[Startup Secrets from the Ramayana]* must read for budding entrepreneurs."

– *The Times of India*

"...[*Superwomen*] unleashes the secret of achieving your passion... perfect combination of emotion and intelligence."

– *Women's Era*

"...[for] youngsters looking for inspiration, this might be the one."

– *Hindustan Times*

"Interesting journey of how 20 women played fantastic roles
towards perfection..."

– *Millennium Post*

"This book encourages entrepreneurship in the youth..."

– *Hindustan*

KAKORI

The Train Robbery that Shook the British Raj

PRACHI GARG

An imprint of
Srishti Publishers & Distributors

Srishti Publishers & Distributors
A unit of AJR Publishing LLP
212A, Peacock Lane
Shahpur Jat, New Delhi – 110 049
editorial@srishtipublishers.com

First published by Bold,
an imprint of Srishti Publishers & Distributors in 2022

10 9 8 7 6 5 4 3 2 1

This is a work of non-fiction based on the author's research through journals, newspaper records, books, personal diaries and interviews with subject experts. While due care has been taken by the author and publisher to verify content at press time, any inadvertent miss that is brought to their notice shall be duly verified and updated subsequently.

Printed and bound in India

Dedicated to
all those revolutionaries
who laid their lives
to see an Independent India.

Acknowledgements

This book has been possible due to the enormous love and support that people have given to me. It was their constant support that kept me going and ensured that I should be able to deliver it on time. I would like to thank everyone for making the journey smooth for me.

Family members play a great role to make such accomplishments possible. In my case as well, this holds true. Each one of them has been instrumental and has been there when required. Special thanks to my father Brijesh Garg and my mother Neeru Garg.

Mr Arup Bose from Srishti Publishers for his faith in my concept and agreeing to publish the same.

Stuti and Vini, my editors, who undertook the tedious task of going through my manuscript, editing it and coming out with exciting ideas.

-: *Acknowledgements* :-

All my friends who provided me with constant moral support to make this happen.

All the readers of *Superwomen, SuperCouples, Supersiblings, The Legends of a Startup Guy, Startup Secrets from the Ramayana* and *Ganesha's Global Startup,* whose love inspired me to venture into the breathtaking historical events of *Kakori*.

Prologue

"है लिए हथियार दुश्मन ताक में बैठा उधर
और हम तैयार हैं; सीना लिए अपना इधर
खून से खेलेंगे होली, गर वतन मुश्किल में है
सरफ़रोशी की तमन्ना, अब हमारे दिल में है।"

(The enemy waits there with weapons, and here we are ready to take their bullets on our chest. We will shed blood if the nation is in trouble; the feeling of sacrifice is now in our hearts.)

I am Ram Prasad Bismil. People know me as a businessman, a poet and a freedom fighter.[1] You may have stumbled upon my readings under the name of Bismil, Ram or Agyat.

---

1. https://indianexpress.com/article/who-is/who-is-ram-prasad-bismil-freedom-fighter-poet-5774792/).

–: *Prologue* :–

I don't know if you have heard my name yet. But if you have, it means the stories of our struggle to get independence for India have reached you. I also hope that you are reading this in independent India, which is my most cherished dream.

I hope you are immensely proud to being a citizen of your country. The nation is home to such a vibrant culture, and a history of struggle. Don't ever take any of this for granted. Freedom was not given to us on a silver platter. My companions and I toiled beyond our capacities to liberate our motherland from the shackles of British rule.

As you soak in the breeze of your free nation, I would like to take you back in time, to the pre-independent era. While I am aware that your history is filled with heroic stories of the freedom struggle, I'm here to elaborate on a defining event which may have slipped the focus of mainstream narratives. Though it might seem like a small incident, it has been pivotal in bringing a revolution across the nation. Through a span of these pages, I will share my journey of participating in the freedom struggle which transformed my life. My intent is to share my life lessons so that you can take inspiration from my experiences and move forward stronger.

If you are sitting in independent India, you must have heard of the heroes who fought courageously in the Indian freedom struggle. I am not sure if I feature in that list, but I can guarantee that I have had the honour of working with a lot of these brave heroes.

-: *Prologue* :-

Let me tell you about all these incredible people who gave up everything for the country.

•

Heroes are not born. It takes years of learning and unlearning involving hardships, conflicts and failures before glory comes to light. It is almost amusing how we are only surrounded by the stories of success, but rarely are told about their most difficult moments which make our heroes more real.

The first struggle for freedom that involved a large number of people came up in 1857. As a result, a full-fledged struggle for independence was brewing when I was growing up. In fact, in the beginning of 1900s, a lot of action was happening as political leaders wanted to come together for more active participation in the governance of the country.

I am sure you will be surprised to know that the initial conversation was not about attaining independence at all. The Congress leaders were hoping to secure a cooperative co-governance of sorts with the British government. But due to a series of failures and disappointments, their demands changed, which gave rise to an organised war of independence.

As I write this, it has been well over a century that the British have established themselves as a permanent rule in our motherland. While our leaders are struggling to have a say in the matters of their country's governance, the British Raj is strengthening their hold by setting up institutionalised assets. I have witnessed the growth of the railways, post offices, educational institutes and governance bodies which was carried out in full swing by the government to give an impression that the country was advancing under their rule.

I see these signs of progress. But does development hold any significance if it is given at the expense of our rights and liberties? What will we do with these luxuries if we are discriminated against on our very soil!

The general dissatisfaction around the mistreatment of the people is growing as a prominent contrast. It is very prominent in the way the so-called lower class people are treated by the British. These seemingly innocuous episodes of discrimination are leading to a rise of angst amongst my people which culminate into these acts of violent protests.

When I look around and observe the plight of my fellow countrymen, my heart bleeds!

The youth has never been so angry. The peasants are in their worst condition. The country looks up to leaders like Mohandas Karamchand Gandhi. Though he has stepped into full-blown activism, he firmly believes in continued goodwill and cooperative relationship with the British. A proponent of non-violence and peace, he is championing for a more collaborative arrangement, with inclusion and active participation of Indian members in the government bodies. Most of the leaders whose voices are heard wish to unite the country under the British Raj.

The British philosophy of setting up an infrastructure reflects their intention to stay as the ruling empire and make a long term base in the country. But there are some who perceive it as a means of progressive development for the Indian population as well.

I don't know what you feel about it, but his approach does not resonate with my sensibilities.

My country is my home and I do not want to serve anyone. I believe in the capability and integrity of my countrymen and refuse to bow down to a foreign master!

Let's understand that when you come from a state of poverty, you would naturally believe that the establishment of better government infrastructure like the railways, post offices, educational institutes, schools and municipal corporations make your life better.

I understand that leaders like Gandhi have travelled widely and possess a wealth of knowledge. He has been able to envisage a progressive environment for the country. Prominent leaders like him were extremely inclined towards a non-violent and symbiotic alliance with the British. But I did not have a lot of faith in the intentions of the government. No matter how "cooperative" it may be on the outside, there will always be an implicit hierarchy which will place us in an inferior position.

I barely had access to privileged education in a global environment, which a lot of my rich counterparts did. Even though I lacked the resource, I did not lack the determination to grow and excel. I was majorly self-taught as I tried to read as much as I could through debate and dialogue about current politics. I was always looking out for media reports and publications so that I could enhance my understanding of what was going on in and outside the country.

Around this time, I got to know about people in the British force, who were more like diplomats, who were more empathetic than some of the privileged Indians. Edwin Samuel Montagu and Lord Chelmsford were some of the men in power who had been active advocates of promoting policies in favour of local governance. They endorsed inclusion of Indians in all possible domains of administration, not only for the purpose of easy operations within the country, but also because it felt like the logical and sustainable way forward to continue their rule peacefully. Given the state of cooperation and participation which was rendered by the educated, upper class of the country, envisaging the collaborative form of governance had not seemed unlikely. However, it was a very myopic perception, as people like me – who did not have come from a position of privilege – were neither given a space for dialogue in this matter, nor taken into consideration.

•

It doesn't take a lot of effort to see that not everything was good under the foreign rule. Casteism and classism was rampant. Since power and money resided in the hands of a few, it was a common cause for dissatisfaction and anger, especially in the commoners. The British were clear about wanting to divide and rule. The conscious division of people along the lines of caste, class and religion was propagated for the rule's benefit.

What followed was quite expected. There was civil unrest and protests in different states. Though not as a national revolution, they existed in pockets with unorganised sects, with different, albeit overlapping agenda. Since such mutinies were localised and planned around specific matters, they only resulted in short-lived effects and failed to create a lingering impact.

As expected, this angered the government quite a bit, even though they did not want to admit it. More importantly, instances in Punjab, Bengal and even in Uttar Pradesh made their way into publications and newsletters, thereby coming into the knowledge of the common masses.[2]

I have always believed in the power of words as it has the potential to create a social revolution. When I got to know about these disruptions, I wrote diligently about the ongoing struggle and exploitation, bringing out publications and articles. By themselves, these instances were not able to create any immediate impact, mostly resulting in death,

---

2. *The Revolutionary:* The final plunge, The wider organisation.

imprisonment and violent oppression of the mutineers. But as a result, a collective wave of consequences was set into motion. These instances stood out as opportunities for people to connect and organise their thoughts and actions.

There's no denying that this was also a very difficult time for world politics. The First World War had placed England and its empire in a difficult position. That was one of the reasons why political strategies in our country were reset to suit the English landscape. With this, the equation between the Indian leaders – who had so far been in the good books – and the British, changed drastically. Although Gandhi had envisaged an inclusive future, the repressive methodology being adopted by the British to curb even the most fundamental rights and consequential protests were a huge setback for a cooperative relationship with the Indian population.

Did you know that several Indians were forced to take part in the World War and their lives were sacrificed! As many as 1.3 million Indian soldiers were forced to serve in the First World War, and over 74,000 of them were lost to death[3].

Sadly, the returning favours were not only unfair, but outright despicable. With the resources of the British heavily focussed towards the war, they had come down with zero

---

3. https://www.indiatoday.in/education-today/gk-current-affairs/story/indian-army-s-unsung-role-and-sacrifices-in-world-war-i-1398762-2018-11-29

tolerance policies towards any kind of civil disobedience in the country. In order to impose law and order, the forces began to exercise arbitrary actions, enforcing punishments without trial, violence even against peaceful workers and dismissal of any pleas brought forth by the Indian leaders.

If we thought that the Empire had been brutal on the downtrodden before, this phase showed us a new low. I knew this was coming. I never believed in their superficial concern, which they portrayed in the guise of infrastructural development. Their true intent was slowly getting revealed.

In fact, this oppressive approach ultimately backfired for the British Raj in India. This autocratic enforcement became a major cause of estrangement and ultimately led to a breach of patience and trust in the common masses, revolutionaries and political leaders alike. In fact, people like me, who had been against the alliance, were getting more eager to find a window to launch the full protest against the British.

However, Gandhi had kept himself uninvolved in protests, till the end of the First World War. At the end of the war, the Montagu-Chelmsford Report[4] recommended introducing controlled levels of self-governance. It would have been a massive step for the Indian leaders to gain

4. Prepared in 1918, presented to the British government on the situation of the governance in India.

some level of participation and control in the management of the country.

But to my utter dismay, this report was completely disregarded. The imposition of the Rowlatt Acts in early 1919 enforced and extended the extreme emergency measures that had been practised during the World War.

And trust me when I say this, you don't want to imagine what this led to!

Several cases were tried without a jury. There was violent retaliation by the forces against any action. It almost felt like they were mocking us while crushing our dreams of power under their feet.

At this point, I am not going to shy away from expressing the irony of the situation. Our leaders had strategically demonstrated a very tolerant outlook towards the British administration. There were several members of the British administration who whole-heartedly supported our progressive participation in everyday governance. However, the Rowlatt Act became a deliberate blow in the face of all our hard work and dedication.

What came forth as our retaliation was the exact opposite of what this act aimed to achieve. It could no longer keep civil unrest under control. Interestingly, most of the Congress leaders would have helped to keep the people of the nation in check, had the British governance followed the recommendations of the Montagu-Chelmsford report.

So I consider this to have been a blessing in disguise, the final nail in the coffin for the British-Indian relationship.

It pushed even the most elite population into a fit of unrest and pulled them out of their illusions. Most importantly, it compelled leaders like Gandhi into rethinking their whole strategy and approach towards the Raj.

Until then, Gandhi led a school of thought which projected the Indian revolution for independence as a peaceful movement, with non-violence and rational demands for inclusion at its core. But, the way this was intended to go – through a unified projection of non-violence in all acts of the protest – was disrupted massively.

It boils my blood to think of the grossly infamous Jallianwala Bagh massacre on 13 April 1919, where hundreds of peaceful, unarmed fellow Indians were shot to death and severely injured. I was shocked to see the extent to which the Raj could go to secure their power and authority.

This cut down the hopes of cooperation, and the façade of the British Raj was finally unveiled! I am happy to say that it broke Gandhi's resolve to stay out of the active politics of the revolution. This was when he launched the Satyagraha movement. This was also when the first organised action was started to mobilise the masses with peaceful protests. As a response to the Rowlatt Act and the shootout at Jallianwala Bagh, a nationwide non-cooperation movement was launched under the leadership of Gandhi. I was thrilled to join the movement wholeheartedly and worked hard to mobilise the youth across the country. I believed it was for the first time that people were seeing a unified direction towards winning freedom.

The one condition that formed the foundation of Gandhi's active leadership in this movement was that we should all adhere to non-violence, boycotting all things British, including services, products and participation. This was a philosophy that resonated well with all of us. It made sense and also uplifted the spirit of *swadeshi,* using all things Indian. The movement went on successfully for a period of almost two years, and as young revolutionaries, we followed it without questioning.

There were times when we felt we were running out of patience, not being able to see any action that the leaders of more radical schools had projected – the more militarily inclined direction like those of the Italian Patriot Mazzini, or even the Russian Revolution and revolutionaries like Catherine Breshkovsky.[5]

During that time, I was fortunate enough to be around the younger generation of freedom fighters. These were my comrades, brothers and friends who supported me in all stages of my struggle. Ashfaqullah Khan, Rajendra Lahiri, Thakur Roshan Singh, Chandra Shekhar Azad, and later,

---

5. https://thewire.in/history/ramprasad-bismil-ideology.

Bhagat Singh were heavily influenced by the directed non-cooperation movement started by Gandhi.

To enhance our understanding of the political scenario, we would discuss the pros and cons of the movement and compare it with the other struggles of independence across the country.

However, the non-cooperation movement did not go as planned. It shifted the curve of progress for the war of Indian independence drastically. There were several sects of revolution rising around us. While the Muslim Khilafat Movement was also intended to align itself with the non-cooperation movement, a sudden violent act crumbled all the efforts to the ground.

A peaceful march of protestors in Chauri Chaura in Eastern Uttar Pradesh was attacked by the police in February 1922, leading to some deaths. At a time when our patience was already being tested, the fire in our hearts was already raging with all the brutality we were being subjected to, such an attack broke all control.

A mob went ahead and burnt down a police station, leading to the death of about twenty policemen. This incident brought the non-cooperation movement to a standstill. Gandhi was extremely disappointed and withdrew the non-cooperation movement overnight, without any discussion with the other leaders.

His lack of willingness to negotiate with us left us in a complete sense of dejection. So many young people of the country had, for the first time, found some direction. But with this sudden withdrawal, the youth wing suddenly became directionless and disoriented as they had given up their education to be a part of the revolution.

•

During this critical time, I used to get letters from young brothers and sisters every day, asking me what they should do next. People visited me to get some guidance on how they should go on with the revolution, while this complete detachment from the earlier intention of participatory coalition with the British Raj was bringing a promising change to the revolution. On the other hand, due to this lack of direction, the movement broke down into sects based on different schools of thought. This divide was becoming more prominent with the passage of time. Senior leaders either did not care or were completely ignorant of the fact that leaders of different philosophies were figuring out their approach for moving forward.

The overall scenario of the independence struggle was gaining momentum. It was headed towards concrete plans, including sorting out the priorities, mobilising people across geographies and gathering all kinds of resources to contribute towards the struggle. However, with the rising level of participation, disillusionment was also becoming a part of the political landscape. Irrespective of the glorified stories you may hear, I must tell you that this was a phase of utter chaos for the country.

With the rising levels of awareness, our appetite for exploration and political activism was on a rapid rise. I am proud to say that at the fundamental level, most of these actions were still based on the principles of non-cooperation and non-violence, irrespective of which sect was working towards it.

But what couldn't be ignored anymore was the desperation that had emerged from inaction! Gandhi's refusal for dialogue, along with rising frustration amongst my friends and comrades!

With the rising uproar, the British suppression of even the most peaceful of protests showed no signs of simmering down. And despite several advocates on the British side, in favour of allowing local governance, the British Raj continued with its autocratic oppression. On account of the failure of the non-cooperation movement, Gandhi withdrew himself from active participation and instead, began focusing on promoting education and swadeshi practices at the grass-root level.

I don't know whether I felt more betrayed by his silence or was more grateful for the fact that he stepped down. Reality is that it was his absence that pushed us towards taking the steps that we did.

It is debatable whether pulling back of the non-cooperation movement brought a massive drop in the flux of the revolution.

But I am sure of one thing, it was an undisputed trigger which led to the rise of the youth around me. We became proactive and lit the fire for uniting the country once again. So many of us, who had been playing in the background and only following orders, now took charge. There is no doubt that several heroes were born and history was created in ways that changed the future of India.

During this time, various political leaders were still aligned with the common principle of Swaraj. But the rising differences were setting several waves of revolution into motion. A lot of this was inspired by the French Revolution and the philosophies of Lenin, from leaders of the world who had liberated their country from the colonial rule and brought it into a state of sustained self-governance.

We had finally opened ourselves to global philosophies that had so far not been considered. Moreover, this was the time when multiple individuals were merging together to become a part of the larger revolution.

•

I am sitting here in a small cell of the jail now. I may not be able to do much, but I am hopeful that my comrades will take this struggle to victory.

If you are wondering how I ended up behind the bars, then just be with me as I will share with you an important part of my life which was pivotal in the struggle for freedom.

Seeing the situation that I have just talked about, agitated and rebellious, my comrades and I were tired of being silent, helpless participants in the struggle for freedom. The very decision to take matters into our own hands and to rewrite the destiny of the youth of the country shook the foundations of the nation.

No matter what the consequences, I am so proud and happy with the life-changing steps we took to bring about an action-oriented plan, a slap in the face of the British Empire. Nothing remained the same since then, but it was worth every single moment of struggle. If I could, I would go back and do this for my country many times over!

Read these pages to know how we went on to fight for our dream. Many of us have taken a stand against many atrocities of the British Raj as well as the silent tolerance of the Indian leaders. We struggled tirelessly against our fears and limitations to not only set things in motion for the young revolutionaries, but also inspire the sleeping nation to rise to the urgency of fighting for our precious freedom.

“नौजवानो! यही मौका है उठो खुल खेलो,
खिदमते-कौम में जो आए बला सब झेलो,
देश के वास्ते सब अपनी जवानी दे दो,
फिर मिलेंगे न ये माता की दुआएँ ले लो”

-: *Prologue* :-

(Youths! This is your chance, get up and play openly,
Bear all that comes in the community,
Give your youth for the country
You may not meet again, take this mother's blessings.)

– Ram Prasad Bismil

1

Youth for Freedom

"मुझे विश्वास है कि मेरी आत्मा मातृभूमि तथा उसकी दीन संतति के लिए नए उत्साह और ओज के साथ काम करने के लिए फिर लौट आएगी।"

(I am sure that my soul will return to work with renewed vigour for the motherland and its humble progeny.)

There are several simple yet momentous instances in life that change the way we think. Moments like these show up as opportunities. Thereafter, it depends on us, whether we have the capability to use this opportunity as our awakening or to let it go.

In the early 1900s, when India was recovering from the baggage of England's wounds in the World War, several people were beginning to get disillusioned. All the false promises that the situation in our country would improve soon were now being washed away. There was lack of faith, understanding and synchronicity amongst our leaders in their principles and practices. Even among the leadership, there was no consensus towards a constructive approach for securing the future of the country.

Amidst this massive distrust, especially after the distasteful failure of strategies by leaders like Gandhi, there was enough unrest that made freedom fighters experiment with new ways to move forward. Gandhi's non-cooperation movement had brought several people together, despite their differences of opinion. Especially the youth of the country, that had been struggling with anger towards the arbitrary control and acts of violence by the British forces. Gandhi's principles of truth and non-violence had struck the right chord with the younger generation of freedom fighters, who were eager to participate towards the new-found goals of creating a nation, free from the British Raj.

It was perhaps the first time since the first war of independence in 1857 that the country was coming together in such an organised manner.

However, Gandhi's sudden withdrawal of the non-cooperation movement without discussion with other leaders had left revolutionaries disheartened. Out of these were the dynamic members of the Hindustan Republican Association (HRA)[6], who had been supporting Gandhi's Satyagraha movement. Leaders like Vallabhbhai Patel had, in turn, influenced freedom fighters across generations, propagating the same principles of non-violence and non-cooperation against the British Raj.

Convincing large masses of hot-blooded youth to conform to such principles had not been an easy task. It is for this reason that young leaders like Bismil and Azad deserve fair credit for having mobilized the members of HRA.

After the withdrawal of the non-cooperation movement, reactionary events were bound to happen. What helped was the farsightedness of the likes of Bismil, Roshan Singh and Lahiri, who got into an actionable mode of mobilizing the frustrated youth and channel their energy into a constructive direction.

Popular belief tells us that the Hindustan Republican Association was full of young blood that acted impulsively and only advocated brute force as a means to shake up British governance. Contrary to popular belief that portrays the youth

---

6. Founded by Ram Prasad Bismil, Ashfaqulla Khan, Sachindra Nath Bakshi, Sachindranath Sanyal and Jogesh Chandra Chatterjee.

of HRA as impatient revolutionaries, the leading members of the HRA were extremely educated people, who were well-versed with world politics. They were excellent orators and writers.

On the other hand were many leaders of the Congress, who were unaware of the larger strategies of politics and the history of colonial war. It is then that leaders like Ram Prasad Bismil, Chandra Shekhar Azad, and Bhagat Singh dedicated themselves towards creating a legacy through literature despite their humble beginnings. It went on to transform the present revolutionary movements in the country tremendously, alongside leaving records of achievements, struggles and thoughts for the future generations.

What is interesting to note is that most of the people who became a part of the HRA came from modest beginnings. It is not far from the truth that even at their tender age, the leading members of the HRA had already seen more struggles compared to the educated, foreign-returned men and women who ruled the Congress. What made the stories of these revolutionaries more relatable was the trigger that brought them onto the path of this struggle for independence.

•

Ashfaqulla Khan was only a child in school when he was exposed to the concept of freedom struggle. A freedom fighter Raja Ram, who was one of those people who circulated and printed books that were originally banned by the British government, was hiding in Ashfaq's school. He was betrayed and reported by an informer. The police came to arrest him at the premises. Ashfaq witnessed this capture along with his schoolmates which left a deep impression in his mind[7].

Under the superfluous understanding of the struggle for independence, Ashfaqulla had watched this arrest and felt that this was a legitimate act by the British Raj. However, when one of his batch-mates expressed dissatisfaction at the unfairness of the arrest of a freedom fighter, Ashfaqulla had jokingly said that he would report the friend to the police as well and get him arrested. The response that he received shook Ashfaqulla to the core.

The young mind could not comprehend what the deep sentiments towards the nation were. Even at that tender age, Ashfaqulla's friend claimed that he would be proud to be arrested for his country. The young Ashfaqulla was profoundly moved by this gesture. He got a glimpse of what it meant to fight for his country. That is also when he understood what honour and privilege this would bring along.

Later, he was introduced to the writings of Walter Scott, through his poetry, "Love of Country" and also the story of Horatius by his teacher. This is where he realised how literature has the power to impact the mind, heart and soul.

---

7. https://www.youtube.com/watch?v=p3txH75FRTs

Thus began his inclination of participation in the struggle for independence.

•

If we talk of Ram Prasad Bismil, we will notice how he came from a household that had seen intense depravity and hunger. But it did not prevent him from being a self-taught scholar who read scraps of paper to educate himself about the political scenario about him. At a very young age, he had already started reading journals and newsletters that covered stories of struggles of people who worked for the independence of the country.

In the course of gaining information, Bismil began to follow the story and trial of Parmanand, a freedom fighter who had been involved in the Lahore Conspiracy Case. He was deeply moved by Parmanand's passion and patriotism for the country. However, when the final verdict came out and Parmanand was sentenced to death, it broke Bismil's heart. It was tough for him to believe that such earnest efforts of fighting for the independence of one's own country would be rewarded in such a brutal manner. Out of anger, Bismil decided to pursue the struggle, and met with Congress members at the convention in Lucknow.

Bismil was also responsible for changing the perception around documentation which was as an important part of the freedom struggle. Such was his thirst for knowledge that he often preferred to go hungry in return for gaining good literature that would increase his understanding of world history and politics.

•

Another striking role model in the freedom struggle was Bhagat Singh, who crossed several boundaries and broke several stereotypes to rebrand the image of a hero. Bhagat Singh was a first-hand victim of the Jallianwala Bagh massacre, which had filled him with the sense of vengeance against the British Empire. At a very young age, Bhagat Singh had started reading informative articles and newsletters. Not just that, he also wrote for journals like *Chand, Prabha, Pratap* and *Kirti,* which inspired people all over the country. He documented all of his experiences and learnings as he wanted to create a valuable asset for the future.

•

Chandra Shekhar Azad, who was deeply inspired by Gandhi, was an outstanding orator. He came from a poor family and was told that if he became adept in Sanskrit, it would improve his social standing. For this purpose, he travelled all the way to Banaras (now, Varanasi), which was a very active community of rising revolutionaries of varied generations. It was here that he came in contact with Bengali revolutionaries and began participating actively. It was through this connection that he came in touch with Ram Prasad Bismil and became a regular member of the troop. Later, he paved the way for setting the wheels of revolution into motion for the HRA. In fact, he was involved with both generations of the revolution – Bismil and Bhagat Singh.

At one instance, when Chandra Shekhar Azad was arrested and ordered to be beaten, after each hit he said, "*Gandhi ji ki jai!*

When asked what his name was, he said "Azad", which means free.

When asked where he lived, he said, "Jail!"

When Ashfaqulla and Bismil died, the HRA merged with the Naujawan Party of Bhagat Singh and later, Chandra Shekhar became the commander in chief for Hindustan Socialist Republican association (HSRA).

•

When Bismil came to the Congress conference seeking guidance for the youth that was eager to contribute to the freedom struggle of the country, he was met with dejection at the lack of willingness by Gandhi or other leaders to engage with him after the recall of the non-cooperation movement. Gravely affected by this indifference, he was compelled to take matters into his own hand and build an open space for the youngsters of the country to unite together and work towards effective results.

It is also true that not all members of the HRA believed in a similar approach towards independence and how the war should be fought. While some believed in hitting the hammer head-on with arms and ammunition, others – still deeply inspired by the principles of Gandhi – felt that the revolution must be continued without provocation and violence. But despite their differences, the members of the HRA maintained a very strong sense of camaraderie and respect, not only for each other, but for freedom fighters across the country. It can be seen in the fact that even though the HRA leaders were disappointed because of Gandhi's decision of recalling the non-cooperation movement, they did not resort to violence. They deliberately refrained from creating an environment that would be counter-productive to the image of Satyagraha.

In fact, there had been instances of petty crimes and thefts all across the country, because without the backing of the resources of Congress, the HRA volunteers were devoid of resources which could support the expenses of publications, travel, accommodation, food and ammunitions.

After the failure of the non-cooperation movement, there was a marked increase in instances of violent protests. Although it was directed primarily against the British, it did show its impact on the Indian citizens, especially in cases of theft or robbery. As soon as it came to Bismil's notice, he called for a discussion and expressed his deep regret against this approach, declaring an immediate ban for any such petty crimes to be directed against the Indian citizens.

2

Hindustan Republican Association

"दुनियाँ से गुलामी का मैं नाम मिटा दूँगा,
एक बार ज़माने को अज़ाद बना दूँगा।"

(I will erase the name of slavery from the world,
I will make the world free once.)

The whole troop was disappointed, just as much as I was. Perhaps more!

We had been working really hard over the last few months to bring together the youth of the country. We had left no stone unturned to gather resources and mobilise the community towards the non-cooperation movement. We gave our all to fan this fire for attaining independence.

When we had shortage of money, my mother was extremely supportive. She was one of the root funders of the initial revolutionary mobilisation. I was determined to create a movement of collective intelligence and informed rationale by enlightening young individuals. I felt that if they are well-versed with the general dynamics of world politics and are aware of the micro-universe, they would be able to understand the freedom struggle better. It definitely helped to have everyone on the same page.

With this intention, I had decided to start with publishing books to earn some money and channelize the resources for creating awareness. Through *How America Won Freedom* by William Luson Thompson and Mrs. E Burrows (1863), I was able to comprehend the political struggle of America and the nuances of their freedom struggle. I knew that this would be intellectually stimulating for the youth of our country. At the same time, the sales of the published book would also help to generate funds that would be needed to support the movement.

This idea was a huge success and within a short span, I was able to recover the amount my mother had lent us and even sustain profit which was sufficient to mobilise people. Many of my comrades had reached out, with their observations from the book, expressing their enthusiasm to work together in the freedom struggle. We still had some books remaining to sell, but this felt like an encouraging idea.

The next step was to produce literature which was readily available and accessible for the youth. This could be a defining step in the circulation of revolutionary ideas.

We published a pamphlet titled "A Message to my Countrymen" which revolved around the arrest of Pundit Gendalalji, a revolutionary who had played an important role in mobilising the population. This pamphlet was well-received and increased the vigour amongst the youth.

In the several districts where this literature was distributed, more young men and women started joining the movement with newfound zeal. Of course, the news spread far and wide and soon, the book and the pamphlet were banned by the United Province.[8]

When Bapu[9] had declared the intention of the non-cooperation movement, we had all felt a strong sense of purpose. We reconfigured our own ideas and thoughts to match the principles of non-cooperation and non-violence.

---

8. Corresponding to the combined regions of present-day Uttar Pradesh and Uttarakhand.

9. A term of endearment used for Mahatma Gandhi by fellows and followers, considering his age and expertise in the political movement.

I also believed in this plan and ideology. Even during my days of struggle, while escaping police or trying to bring the banned book into the Congress Convention, some members of the group advised me to eliminate potential threats. We had been moving under a lot of stress and it was often that we were caught off-guard, without protection or money. It was a challenging time and though I would have wanted more from them, I couldn't blame them for showing weakness of nerves. And yet, despite the vulnerability, I never agreed to kill anyone, such was my reverence for Bapu's philosophy.

And yet, he didn't consider us worthy enough to even discuss the withdrawal of the non-cooperation movement! I understand that the Chauri Chaura incident was not in our favour. It projected the revolutionaries in a negative light in front of the larger world audience.

But this is a country full of diversity. It is ambitious, albeit not unrealistic, to bring everyone on the same page. It is unfair to label any one kind of behaviour as the general representation of the masses. I could sense the angst in the hearts and minds of the youngsters who had put everything at stake to contribute towards the larger cause of the motherland.

Quite frankly, I could sense that this withdrawal was beginning to show more aggressive consequences, which ironically it had originally intended to stop. So many people had begun writing to me as they wanted convincing answers.

I could see that these young revolutionaries were beginning to get flustered.

And I am not just talking about letters. There were speeches, protests and even reactionary responses to this unpredictable move which punctured the momentum of the freedom struggle. Little acts of thefts against anyone in power were visible from the periphery. Though these were arbitrary instances of violence, I did not like the turn of events. The leaders, whom I admired, had turned their backs towards us. But I couldn't do the same to all those who looked up to me. The way they were reaching out to me showed that they wanted a definite path to follow.

Soon, we found ourselves knee-deep in impulsive, multi-forked actions rooted in different objectives. If this went on, all thc effort of mobilising the youth would be futile. This had to be put to a stop. Finally, I was hoping to see how we could solve this tricky situation.

Despite our ideological and philosophical differences, we were all connected by a common thread of unity and brotherhood. All revolutionaries from across the country kept a close watch on each other's progress and safety. Despite Bapu's refusal to discuss the withdrawal of the movement, I was determined to find a solution. It had to be something that we could all agree upon so that we could all move forward collectively. Thus, I went to the Congress Convention in Gaya to find a solution The entire senior leadership of Congress and several other prominent members were there.

To me, this looked like a potential opportunity to reconvene the plan and work backwards from the withdrawal of the non-cooperation movement. However, our requests were met with blank refusals. Our presence was not even acknowledged, so we could not present our point of view. This really broke our spirits as we saw our dream of attaining independence for our beloved country crumbling down.

I realised that the Congress had become an organisation which was dominated by the rich. The wealthy revolutionaries had primarily become office-bearers and were making all the decisions.

From whatever I could gather, I was aware that the quality was declining, the agenda was falling apart and volunteers were struggling to make ends meet. As all support withdrew, youngsters who had been working across districts became more restless and desperate. Many of them, who came from humble backgrounds, were reaching out to me, asking for money even for basic sustenance. There were only so many loans and favours we could have asked for. I was really disheartened to see that the glorious leaders, whom we had relied on, trusting the future of the country, were becoming so inactive and unfocussed in their own approach.

In placing our leaders on a pedestal, we forgot that they were human beings with flaws and personal grievances. For a country which was struggling for independence, there was no scope for error. I did not realise when the senior leaders withdrew their support for the youth. They were now turning to me and my comrades for direction. We were expected to have it together, but to be in that position is both humbling and unnerving.

•

I had been an Arya Samaji[10] from a very early age in my life. This sect of Hinduism follows sincere devotion and requires strict disciplinarian pursuit for a true follower. I had been fortunate enough to seek guidance under the enlightened Guru Swami Somdev very early on in my life. This conditioning had made me tough, disciplined and focussed.

As far as the inner turmoil was concerned, I was able to tackle it with my principles and values. But, even a sage has a stomach that takes over the strongest of minds. We had mouths to feed and costs to cover. In the stage of revolution where the country's eyes were on us, volunteers were asking for money and offices were shutting down under attack. Our motherland expected us to rise to the challenge, get resources to sell publications and organise conferences, marches and battles. And here we were, struggling for basic amenities!

---

10. Arya Samaj is a reform movement that promotes a way of life based on the tenets of the Vedas.

Upon realising the urgency of the situation, I spent many nights budgeting our ration with my comrades and eating *sattu*[11] because that was all we could afford. My mother had made sure that growing up, I always drank a glass of milk before I went to sleep. But now, even that glass of milk seemed like a luxury to me. Even the thought of consuming it was a sin to me when my brothers and sisters were fighting against poverty.

The rich and privileged political leaders may have broken our hearts, but not our dreams. I decided that it was time for us to break away from this stagnation created due to the indecisiveness of influential political leaders. And thus came into existence our very own body called the Hindustan Republican Association. We worked tirelessly to create the party mandate. We named it the "Revolutionary". Within a few days, with the help of volunteers, we were able to print pamphlets in places like Lahore, Rangoon, Bombay, Amritsar and Calcutta, along with key cities of the United Province. What a shock it had been for the Indian government to know that we had managed to pull this off internally!

This formally marked the decision to digress from the main Congress body, breaking it into two sections. The Swaraj Party, which was led by Motilal Nehru, was the liberal

11. Sattu is a type of flour common in India. It can be cooked as chapattis or as a soup.

sect which followed the principles of non-violence and non-cooperation. On the other hand, we became the rebels. We were a different sect which was open to armed protests as we wanted immediate actions and results.

Soon after its formulation, the organisation was joined by several young revolutionaries and made prominent moves that contributed to the foundation of the last wave of the freedom struggle. The constitution of HRA was formed with the help of Sachindra Nath Sanyal, who also wrote the party's manifesto.[12] The declaration was published on 1 January 1925. It proposed the overthrow of British colonial rule and its replacement with a "Federal Republic of the United States of India". In addition, it sought universal suffrage and the socialist-oriented aim of the abolition of "all systems which make any kind of exploitation of man by man possible."

This broadly covered our aspirations and made our manifesto inclusive, yet achievable. This manifesto also showed us hope against all odds. It helped us conceptualise our independent India.

By breaking away from the Congress and its arbitrary, elitist dictatorship, we lost access to the shelter and obligations

---

12. http://www.worldcat.org/title/hanging-of-ram-prasad-bismil-the-judgement/oclc/219562122&referer=brief_results),whoalsowrote the party's manifesto.

of the patrons. This meant that we were headed towards an uncertain future as we lacked resources.

However, I had complete faith in my organisation. I was proud to be a part of the group which was willing to walk an extra mile to accelerate the fight for independence. The country was in a state of utter chaos and disillusionment. The time had come to reject elitist discussions and promote effective actions which could yield results.

The HRA mostly consisted of young individuals who were connected to their roots. They had closely witnessed the atrocities of the British. Most of us had nothing to lose. With help coming to us from all corners of the country, I felt confident that we were in the right direction.

We were set to roll out the revolution for a free nation!

3

The Plan of the Robbery

"ऐ प्यारे गरीबो! घबराओ नहीं दिल में, हक़ तुमको तुम्हारे, मैं दो दिन में दिला दूंगा।"

(Oh dear poor! Don't worry in your hearts, I will give you your rights in two days.)

Dear reader, are you following my story? Or have you lost interest in the struggles of those who do not make glamourous appearances in newspapers and radio? Is our story still a part of your life?

Of course, there is also a possibility that our stories have been long forgotten and the precious papers on which we poured our hearts are being sold as scraps. But I hope that you have plenty of resources to build a successful and prosperous life. Believe me, for us, abundance and luxury was something we saw only in the lives of Britishers. They thrived on account of our misery.

For those who look from their vantage points of comfort, the lives of revolutionaries only revolve around heroic actions, immortal slogans and majestic marches that shake the world. You will hear ample stories about how battles were won and negotiations were made. Your history books will give you dates and memorials.

However, there is a not so glorious side of heroism in endless dark struggles and miseries which often go undocumented in the tales of valour. For every one individual who makes it to the books or finds their name on posters and calendars, there are a thousand other unsung heroes who work tirelessly and yet do not get acknowledged.

When you hear about the stories of the Hindustan Republican Association, you would probably hear about young revolutionaries who are full of enthusiasm and passion to bring our motherland to its well-deserved fate of independence. But the sad truth is that passion and enthusiasm alone is never enough. As we broke away from the Congress, we also had to let go of the patronage of the elite leaders of the country. So we were on our own, in terms of guidance, decisions and actions. The bitter truth is that we had to scavenge for resources to move forward.

There were many volunteers across the country who had much debt and had to sell their belongings to keep our offices running. I tried hard to lobby with the rich sympathisers across the country. I appealed to their patriotic side to dedicate a certain amount of their earnings to contribute to the cause revolutionaries. I even came up with ingenious ways to collect money by devising a monthly subscription format. But despite all my efforts, nobody paid heed to my request.

As a result, all our funding shrivelled away soon, leaving us with very little to even survive, let alone operate. So many of our offices gradually began shutting down. So many of our volunteers, who had given up their jobs and education for of their love for the nation, were forced to give up and go back to their routine lives. But, I did not give up. I continued to look for money in places where there was even the slightest of possibilities. I begged people to teach me skills and trades that could help me expand my earnings.

But I hate to admit that we were living in dark times where trust was the most expensive resource. People did not want to associate with the revolutionaries to ensure their own safety. It was easy for everyone to talk about the country behind closed doors and express their dissatisfaction. But when it came to active participation and contribution, no one came to our aid. I am deeply saddened to admit that the country failed its revolutionaries!

•

I knew I had to be make hard decisions because there were so many people who were willing to fight alongside me, despite the challenges. Trust me, I did try my best to live up to their expectations. But I am no fool when it comes to admitting my own mistakes. I knew we did not have the experience or the shrewdness, which the senior leaders of Congress had used to mobilise the masses. I realised that we were losing people every single day. It was a difficult choice between freedom and food for their families. It was heartbreaking to lose honest, hard working and sincere people, who were otherwise ready to give their lives for the country.

Often, I put a brave smile and encouraged people to keep moving forward. But there were times when the letters, requests and visits of desperation shook me up. Sometimes, my helplessness used to take the better of me. I broke down a couple of times in front of my comrades. We were so poor that most of us wore torn and worn-out kurtas and dhotis, somehow managing to continue with the work of the HRA.

I am not recalling this phase of misery as a means to dramatize the struggle that my comrades and I went through. The reason I talk about this depravity is because we understand the price that we pay for heroism. I also emphasise on these struggles so that we have a broader context to empathise with the plight of the revolutionaries who had given up so much, not for some selfish goal, but for the larger dream of an independent nation. So when I talk about what happened next, I hope there is more understanding that helps to differentiate between right and wrong.

•

The different ways in which the HRA was functioning resulted in two kinds of consequences. One was that the volunteers started backing out and offices began shutting down, while the other was that people started experimenting with various ways to gather resources so that the struggle for independence could continue. I witnessed an increase in petty thefts and robberies around the country. Since people had exhausted all other means of arranging for money, including asking the so-called 'well-wishers' and trying new trades and businesses, a lot of them felt that this was the last resort. Petty theft of shops and rich people's houses were becoming more common.

I felt that this was wrong on various levels. I knew that this approach was neither going to be successful to obtain short-term results nor the long-term impression that the HRA members wanted to create.

Police atrocities and arrests had been increasing and stronger actions with lower tolerance were becoming the norm. Above all, the defamation that was being caused because of all this was extremely counterproductive for the larger objective of the HRA. I observed this for a while until I could take it no more. We were setting a bad example, and more importantly, causing harm to our fellow Indians. This was not the right step, both ideologically as well as logically, because we were beginning to earn the reputation of being hooligans, who were violent and did not care about social welfare.

At this point, I called a meeting and sent out notices across the organisation, banning any attack on our fellow Indians' life or property. We even included in our manifesto that no Indian life should come to harm in our struggle for independence.[13] This decision was fortunately welcomed unanimously and brought some relief to me, for the moment. I knew this was not going to be a solution for too long, since lack of money and resources was already pushing us to our limits.

•

It was around this time in early 1925 that I was travelling in a train from Shahjahanpur to Lucknow to meet some comrades. I noticed that at every station, the police would

---

13. It was known as Peela Parcha, i.e. the yellow paper. The document can be viewed at The National Archives of India in the Home Department file. The manifesto was released on 1 January 1925.

come and hand over a bag to the train guard. Since I was in the cabin right next to the guard's, I could see that at every station, the bag was collected and put into a metallic chest. This got me curious and I started calculating the possibilities.

With some questioning and snooping around, I found that this was the tax money being collected from every station. Then, it was sent to the government. I started making closer observations about this transaction. I had imagined that when the chest finally reached Lucknow, it would be locked for full security. However, when I got down to see what was happening at the Lucknow station, I saw that there were no locks and chains.

Keeping this observation in mind, I came back and shared everything I had just learnt with my comrades.

Chandra Shekhar Azad, Ashfaqulla Khan, Roshan Singh and Rajendra Lahiri were some of my closest confidants. They heard me attentively as I elaborated on the amount of money which could be procured if we could organise a robbery of the British treasury.

Many members did not agree with my proposal instantly as they were all a part of an organisation which was strictly against any act of violence. They also believed that this would send a very wrong message on behalf of the HRA to the country. There was one more problem. It would bring us in direct and open animosity against the government.

So far, most of us had been working underground. We had not come under the radar of the police so as to arouse any suspicion. This open attack on government property would become an act of defiance. Some believed that it might create a negative image of the revolutionaries by placing us in the same category as robbers or hooligans.

"If we approach this the right way, it can solve all our problems. We are in desperate need for money to sustain the movement," I said, trying to make sense of all these possibilities and expressing my thoughts to everyone.

"Robbing at such a large scale will be a challenge. We will have to plan and ensure that we do not hurt any fellow Indian. We have to stay true to our core values which are there in our manifesto," said Ashfaqulla Khan, lovingly called Ashfaq.

I was happy to see that he understood my perspective well. With this statement, all the doubts and apprehensions vanished. The other members could feel the conviction of our decision and agreed eventually. The fight for independence demanded us to give our all and there was no other way to achieve our dream. Soon, the plan for the Kakori robbery started hatching out.

•

To begin with, we started making calculations and concluded that between Shahjahanpur and Lucknow, with a consistent collection, there could be close to ten thousand rupees in the chest. So if we robbed the train at the Lucknow station, not only would we be able to get a good amount of money, but also not hurt any Indians in this process.

We would be rightfully taking back what belonged to us. After all, this money was forcibly collected taxes from people who could not afford them.

Perception of our countrymen had to be kept in mind for our mission to succeed in the long run. In the end, the robbery was executed for the greater cause of independence. At the HRA, there was no hierarchy in the organisation. Everyone was free to express their opinions without having to worry about offending or displeasing anyone. It had been a conscious decision to set up such an open and conducive culture in the organisation. Because truth be told, the lack of transparency and dialogue were the reasons which drifted us away from the Congress. It was obvious that a few elites had control over all decision-making, both in principle as well as practice. These people governed the direction in which Congress would change at the drop of a hat.

Deliberately steering away from such a culture, the HRA was designed in a manner to promote participation and volunteerism without the fear of hierarchy. We did this to encourage ownership and responsibility amongst all the comrades. It also helped in inculcating a sense of brotherhood. With such an arrangement in place, decisions were made after open discussions. Quite naturally, we could not agree on several issues, but we tried our best to make the operations as democratic as possible. The decision of carrying out the train robbery was also somewhat like this.

Some of my closest friends and comrades had shown hesitation when I first proposed the plan. Keeping my personal motivation aside, I had tried my best to make sure that their concerns were all heard, acknowledged and addressed in the most reasonable manner.

Essentially, there were two motivations that were the driving force behind the plan. The first was that we desperately needed the money to accelerate the movement. The second motivation was to challenge the government. Such an act of fearless defiance that targeted a government property would be a one-of-its-kind event. It would strongly undermine the control of the police and send out a clear message, both to the British Raj as well as to the countrymen, that no amount of depravity would hold us back anymore.

In fact, taking this money that actually belonged to the Indians seemed like a symbolic way to tell the world that the revolutionaries would reclaim the country from the hands of the British.

In a time where even basic meals were a luxury, where we spent time together in the fields, hearing stories of losses all around us, this proposition filled us with a renewed hope. It gave us a sense of direction and allowed us to focus our energies into a plan of action that would give immediate and significant results.

The risks involved were too high, but I felt that my comrades and I were beyond the stage of calculating risks. There was not just desperation to acquire resources for our activities, but the angst to get the revolution rolling. Once the decision for the robbery had been made, I was happy to see that even those who had expressed apprehensions were now completely on board. This was extremely harmonizing for the spirit and energy of the organisation. The first hurdle was crossed and we had a long way to go.

What lay ahead of us next was to meticulously plan the whole strategy in a manner that would be realistic. We would have to minimise the risks as much as possible. With high spirits and dedication, we put our minds together to come up with a powerful plan that would shake this country up and change our present as well as our future.

4

Robbing what was Ours

"हम भी घर के अंदर आराम कर सकते थे, हम भी जीवन का आनन्द ले सकते थे। हमारा भी परिवार है, हम भी किसी के बच्चे हैं, हमें भी अपने माता-पिता ने दर्द और प्यार से पाला है। लेकिन ओह! हम बाहर आते समय उन्हें यह कहना भी भूल गए, जब आंसू निकलकर जमीन से टकराते हैं, तो बस याद रखना, तुम बच्चे अभी भी वहीं हो।"

(We too could rest inside the house, we too could enjoy life. We too have a family, We are also someone's children, we too have been nourished

with pain and love by our parents. But oh! We even forget to say to them while leaving our homes, "When the tears come out and hit the ground, just remember, your child is still there.)

There was excitement and vigour amongst my comrades. After months of struggle, we had something to look forward to. Ever since the withdrawal of the non-cooperation movement, people had become disoriented towards any specific path that would lead us to freedom. There had been a lot of diplomacy and discussion when it came to taking concrete steps in the Congress. I am not saying that there is no rationale behind the way the early leaders of Congress deliberated, but I will not shy away from saying that there were a lot of drawing room conversations which did not lead to any effective action.

On the other hand, whenever some of us tried to suggest a path that could show results, we were dismissed on account of being impractical as our proposals did not resonate with the philosophies of the leading members of the Congress. You can imagine how frustrating it would have been, not just for me but for all the volunteers across districts, who were toiling day and night without any resources. So, when the train robbery plan struck our minds, it appeared to be a powerful way in which we could control the circumstances.

When I look back, I wonder how I became a part of this plan. The people who knew me understood that I was a disciplined Arya Samaji, who lived by the rules of hard work and perseverance. I had dealt with transactions of weapons in my my younger years, but I was not inherently violent.

This revolution meant everything to me, so I wanted to do everything in my capacity to take it to a logical end. I knew what we were planning had never been done before. Once we rolled this plan into action, there would be no turning back.

Sitting here and writing down my memories now, I think back to the time when I was actually in the train, observing the collection of taxes going on nonchalantly between the police and the cabin guard. What felt like a mundane job at every station was a lucrative opportunity for us!

It never occurred to us that the exorbitant amount of taxes collected by the government would be getting transported from one place to another with such little security. It just showed the arrogance of the British, who did not feel the need to secure tax money. Such was their sense of entitlement as they did not even think that a common man could pose any threat to them.

Their over-confidence was not unfounded. Most of us had not taken any daring steps to show our agitation since the revolt of 1857. The Congress had been mostly diplomatic and cooperative. Our leaders wanted to form an alliance with them. They were comfortable in living under the shining boots of the British Empire.

And therefore, the British were not the only ones who have earned my anger. I was very disappointed with our Indian counterparts who had become submissive and complacent with the way the country was being ruled.

It pains me to admit that we were more accepting towards our colonial masters. We did not stand up against the tyrants who had ransacked our treasures and crushed our pride. I don't know why more people did not have the fire of vengeance which propelled them to act in the interest of our nation, just like me and my comrades! There was no point complaining against lifeless statues.

•

With the plan of the train robbery having been floated around amongst the trusted members of the HRA, we began discussing how we could actually implement it.

Between Shahjahanpur and Lucknow, an estimated amount of ten thousand rupees would be collected in the chest in the guard's cabin. If we were to attack the cabin at the Lucknow station, surround the train with armed men and cut down the access between the police and the cabin just long enough to grab the chest and escape, we would be successful in our goal.

By calculating the access that the police would have at the Lucknow station as well as the number of people who would be required to ensure that we were in control of the situation, we concluded that we would need at least thirty people, all well-armed and equipped, to bring us into a position of advantage.

Having said that, considering that the location was Lucknow, it would not be very difficult for reinforcements to arrive at the station if the police were to contain us. Another risk that appeared was that escaping in Lucknow would be challenging, keeping in mind the vast spread of forces and easier tracking. When we analysed the risks in this situation, we concluded that not only would this plan be extremely ambitious, it would also cost us dearly. And despite all this planning, the success of the robbery would not be guaranteed. From that perspective, it felt like there were high chances that we would come out of this situation deeper in debt and losses than we currently were.

But this did not waver our focus. We just had to come up with an alternative which would not put so many people at high risk. It is true that when we collaborate seamlessly and allow the space for dialogue and disagreement, we are able to contribute wholeheartedly. In our meetings also, we were able to push our own thinking capacity to come up with innovative ideas.

In the HRA, my comrades and I tried to break away from conventional thoughts, encouraged dialogues and welcomed disagreement. My closest friend and brother, Ashfaqulla Khan was the perfect example of this. Despite being a strict Arya

Samaji myself, because of Ashfaq's passion and dedication, I was able to break my own shackles of prejudice against Muslims. It was because of his persistence that despite the taunts that he faced within his family and his community, Ashfaq had successfully broken away from the impositions that had prevented Hindus and Muslims to bond and work together in the struggle of independence.

I can clearly recall the disapproval in the eyes and voices of many Hindu comrades when Ashfaq began participating in HRA and eventually started rising to a higher position. There had been many raised eyebrows when he and I started becoming and confidants. And yet, I cannot forget how Ashfaq continued with his loyalty and dedication to give his best in the struggle for independence. He continued to mobilize the Muslim youth around him and eventually managed to change the perspective of both the communities. This was precisely the kind of camaraderie and harmony that we wanted to develop in our organisation.

Ashfaq was not the only one who had earned my unconditional trust. I was lucky enough to be surrounded by people who were passionate about the cause as well as loyal towards the organisation. Rajendra Lahiri, Roshan Singh and Chandra Shekhar Azad are some of those people who I could trust with my eyes closed. And it was these people who I confided in to plan the best way to execute the robbery, without risking our lives.

-: *Kakori* :-

•

Since we all agreed that executing the robbery at the Lucknow station would be potentially life-threatening, we realised that it would not be worth the risk. This is why alternate plans were thought out.

"What if we don't wait for the train to get to the Lucknow station?" I asked as we were developing our strategy for the robbery together.

"What if we do this at a smaller station, where we do not expect a lot of armed policemen?" Ashfaq said, continuing my chain of thought.

I liked his idea of choosing a smaller station. We had to ensure that we were not suspected by the police, so boarding the train from a station where there is less security would keep us safe.

"Why do we have to do this at a station at all? We will only risk more lives at any station, expose ourselves to more witnesses and naturally, any station will have a lot more guards and police than an unsuspecting location in the middle of any two stations," Rajendra Lahiri said.

This made perfect sense! We could easily halt the train by pulling a chain in the compartment and rob the train without anyone even expecting that an attack would happen. This way, the only people who would be involved are the cabin guards and the few policemen who would be on the train.

With multiple perspectives flowing in, things were slowly becoming clearer. Through deliberation, we were able to crystallise our thoughts which helped us figure out what would be a discreet place to execute the robbery.

Having travelled that route several times, I knew that Kakori was a small town, just about sixteen kilometres from Lucknow. It was close enough to facilitate escape and just far enough so that the forces from Lucknow would not be able to reach us at a short notice. Finally, the plan was finalised.

We would rob the Number 8 Down train, travelling from Shahjahanpur to Lucknow. We would do this between Lucknow and Kakori, in a small, uninhabited location. This plan significantly reduced our risk. Stopping the train in the middle of nowhere simply meant that we would not have as many eyes watching us, as we would have on any station. It also meant that we only had the police force already on the train to deal with, along with the train guards.

After due calculation, we concluded that ten men would be sufficient to execute the robbery in this scenario.

I was the one who would face the cabin guards to rob the chest. I knew for a fact that Ashfaq and Azad were also willing to take up this responsibility. But, as a leader, I had to make sure that they were safe. I knew this was a dangerous situation and I could not let anyone else go through that risk while I stood by. They respected my decision and our plan was sealed.

Initially, Azad had was not in favour of the robbery as he had expressed apprehensions against the whole plan. But, seeing our determination, he resolved to support us, no matter what the consequences were. Once we had decided on something, we did not back down. So, when the plan for the Kakori robbery had been finalized, Azad was the first one to nominate himself to be a part of the heist.

Then, we shortlisted ten people who were ready to spearhead the plan. Along with me, it included Rajendra Lahiri, Chandra Shekhar Azad, Sachindra Bakshi, Keshab Chakravarthy, Manmath Nath Gupta, Mukundi Lal, Murari Lal Gupta and Banwari Lal.

The plan was to get on the train in Shahjahanpur and wait till the designated spot near Kakori. That's where the chain would be pulled and we would immediately move on to the guard's cabin to reclaim the chest of money. We would all be armed with weapons, but I was very clear that our motive would not be to hurt anyone, especially civilians. I would announce in the train that we were only here to collect what the government had unjustly taken from us and did not mean any harm to anyone.

It was also decided that those of us who were adept at using weapons would stand close to the guard's cabin and keep firing shots intermittently to make sure that nobody approached that coach. It was also a tactic to create an illusion that the train was heavily surrounded by a large number of armed men.

"What if the chain to stop the train did not work? How would we tackle this situation?" Azad asked.

The distance between Kakori and Lucknow was not enough to be able to get down from one coach to climb into another and then try to halt the train. By the time we managed that, we would be too close to the Lucknow station and this would completely turn the tables to our disadvantage.

After a brief pause, I said, "To solve this problem, let's board the train from both the first class and the second class compartments. So, if one chain fails, the second team could pull the chain in their compartment to make sure the train stops."

We designated tasks to all the participants. Lahiri was to pull the chain, I was to retrieve the chest. Some of us were told to stand outside the train and stop anyone from entering the area close to us. Others were supposed to guard the location and help with crowd management.

"We will not use our weapons in any arbitrary manner. We will only fire to maintain fear in the policemen in the train." I emphasised. While all of us were supposed to carry guns, the rest of us were not to use them. It was also because not everyone was comfortable using weapons. We certainly did not want any additional accident happening out of nervousness.

With the help of some well-wishers, who were finally happy to see that some action was being taken, we were able to manage some resources and money to gather weapons and tickets. We were all going to board the train as individuals so that bi-standers could not identify us as a large group. We also decided to cover our faces during the robbery to avoid being recognised later.

This optimism that came with the planning taught me a great deal about organisation and trust. The way we had planned the robbery gave me a lot of confidence. I felt we had covered all aspects. We were now prepared to do this with minimal risks. In instances like these, when I look back and recall the inputs and observations that my comrades had given, I realise how connected we were to common people and the challenges they face every single day. We strived to find ways to accommodate these challenges and make the path forward easier for everyone.

We knew that this was in sharp contrast to the way things worked in Congress. Most of the key decision-making men came from places of entitlement. At the risk of sounding judgmental, I know that this prevented them from broadening their horizons and gaining experiences that would help them to empathize with the real struggles of the population of the country.

During this journey, I had trusted few people who had stood by me through thick and thin of our struggles. I also trusted their belief systems, which is why I never questioned the people that they themselves had faith in.

–: *Prachi Garg* :–

I will not deny that when lives are at risk, even the strongest walls of trust can break. Still, the stakes were much higher for the country than for us as individuals.

But for now, dear reader, the upcoming robbery was keeping us awake at night. We knew that on 9th August, things would change in a way that they would never be the same again.

5

The Human side of Heroes

"क्या इसी तरह हमेशा भारत माँ के वक्षस्थल पर विदेशियों का तांडव नृत्य होता रहेगा? कदापि नहीं, इतिहास इसका प्रमाण है। मैं मरूँगा किन्तु फिर दुबारा जन्म लूँगा और मातृभूमि का उद्धार करूँगा।"

(Will foreign forces keep ruling and exploiting Mother India? Never! History is proof of this. I will die but will be born again to save the motherland.)

So many plans, so many discussions and so much excitement! Kakori was all we could think about. It was all we talked about when we sat together.

I am sure most of us were dreaming about the heist the whole time. It was obvious as a lot was at stake, not just our lives. The higher priority was the future of the organisation and the country. We were posing a big risk by exposing ourselves. This attack would bring us under the watchful eyes of the police. It would also send out a strong statement that the revolutionaries were out in the open to attack the government. And once the statement had been made, there was clearly no turning back. It would mean that those of us who were involved in the robbery directly or indirectly would have to be under a constant threat of getting arrested. This was going to affect us at many levels.

If we succeeded in the robbery, we would be able to pay off debts and secure some financial stability. This would also mean that a very concrete and path-breaking step would have been taken by the HRA, which could set a precedent for the organisation to follow, and send the strong message to the British government that we were well past the stage of tolerance and cooperation.

What I was really hopeful for, was the wave of emotion it would set in the country, indicating that the revolution had begun in the real sense. This would also be a call to the nation, calling out volunteers and aspirants across the country that a new movement had begun, which would bring them solid actions. This message would help the world to see that as a country, we were united. We had started taking steps towards independence. So far we had been a country that had acted upon diplomacy and fear to a large extent. It was definitely time to change that impression. We had to mark our existence as a capable and strong nation on the world map.

How we felt as an organisation was pretty evident. But how we felt as individuals had many shades to it. As I have pointed earlier, most of us were young students who were on the brink of entering adulthood. A lot of us had no professional training. We barely understood world politics and were not honed strategists. To be honest, some of us had never even fired a shot from a gun.

Reading stories about heroes is bound to make one feel that we were capable and had it all figured out. That's usually how we perceive the image of a hero; we see them as pillars of strength standing on pedestals. Often, we only witness them on public forums, delivering speeches, or in action. They are always in their best shape and form. What we forget about them is that there are also human beings with imperfections, just like us. They have also covered journeys of growth and failure, mistakes and lessons.

That is the kind of problem that I see among the people around me. Anyone who is fighting for the independence of the country is suddenly put on a pedestal with unnaturally high expectations placed on them. I am not saying that heroes don't deserve that respect, but it is important that we accept that all heroes have flaws and weaknesses.

I say this because people whom I revered in this freedom struggle have shown me their weaknesses. People whom I thought were flawless have disappointed me too. I also know that those who have inspired me are themselves quite vulnerable.

My own Guru, Swami Somdev was somebody I looked up to with utmost respect. He was just like god to me; everything he said was my religion. I could never imagine him being vulnerable or weak. That is the kind of image that a hero creates in our minds; we only see them with their super powers and forget about their everyday struggles.

I was with Swamiji towards the end of his life. I had seen his illness, which weakened him. I witnessed his body wither away and watched him struggle every day for survival. Although I know that his illness did not break his spirit; knowledge and love was all around him, even in his most delicate form. But the experience of looking at him in that state and seeing how a strong man can transform into a frail body really shook me up.

Swamiji had believed that yoga was a powerful form of education and meditation, and his knowledge and experience in yoga *asanas* was a treasure in itself. Despite that, towards the end of his life, he had become so weak that he did not even have the strength to explain the forms of yoga that he practiced, let alone performing the asanas himself.

My guru left his worldly form with regret and angst of not being able to share his knowledge of the yoga asanas with his students. The biggest treasure of his wisdom withered away with him. I stood like a helpless and broken bystander who watched him lose his body. That is when I saw the human side of him, in addition to his god-like image that I had in my mind.

I believe that experiences in life are not meant to be consumed in isolation. These experiences are interconnected, creating a wide network of knowledge, that transform and transpire from one instance to another. My experience with Swamiji in his last moments inculcated in me the element of compassion and empathy. It is because of him that I am able to accept the more humane emotions. I believe in accepting the failures of the people who are put on a pedestal.

The reason I talk about this is because, in some way, we had become people who were in a position of power. The ten volunteers of the Kakori robbery had subconsciously put themselves on a pedestal. Not only was the entire organisation looking at us with expectations, but people who knew us, empathised with our cause.

And as glorious as the position of power may seem, it has its downside. It puts you under the spotlight which can be a very unnerving experience. Even though we had prepared meticulously for the robbery, deep down I was scared. I was acutely aware of my vulnerabilities, fears and apprehensions.

I would often think about my mother and wonder how she would feel. My thoughts went back to my friends who had supported me and my cause for the country. I would think back about the people who had made compromises so that people like me would step up and rise to the challenge of fighting for the country. I also thought about my enemies or those who looked at me with disapproval. Most importantly, I would think about my comrades and friends who were standing with me to execute the plan and walk with me till the end.

While we were prepared on the logistics front, with our contingency plans in place, I knew that, just like me, my friends were also going through an emotional roller-coaster ride. I say this out of sheer respect and and humility. We were in sync with our vulnerabilities and emotions.

Most of us had family responsibilities and obligations back home. A lot of us were in debt and yet, all of us were passionately dedicated towards the cause of independence. So, in a way, our past, present and future, all three were on the line.

We had strictly instructed each other to not talk about our plans outside of the core circle. But I understood that we were all looking for support and sympathy. Some of us were able to provide that to each other through motivational conversations and discussions. We would sing songs, read books, do physical exercises or simply engage ourselves with activities that helped us calm down. While we might be hesitant to show our vulnerable side to each other beyond a point, we all longed for some reassurance and solace.

It was during this stage that some of my friends made observations about a few people who they thought were a little too sensitive. They said that these people could potentially be the weaker links of our chain. Since their vulnerability could have deeper implications, our concern was not just that they would not be able to cope with the situation. Our bigger concerns were that they might pose a risk to the operation by doing something that could compromise our success, as well as the safety and security of the team.

So, dear reader, when I say that there was a lot at stake, I hope you understand the severity of the situation. When I look back at those times and assess my reaction, I realise that I was lacking in experience and insights. I didn't quite understand all the perspectives. I did not fathom the extent of the threat. And I did not evaluate what would happen if the weaker links of our chain broke down in front of the British government.

Was I arrogant? Was I short sighted? Was I so consumed by my enthusiasm that I did not understand the deeper realities of the situation? Most importantly, was I the exact portrayal of how the elder leaders perceived the young revolutionaries to be?

I try not to be too harsh on myself and my friends now. I strongly believe that our intentions were right and we did everything in our capacity to make sure that our goals were successful. But I do humbly acknowledge that if I were to turn back and try to plan the whole thing all over again, I would rely more on my experience and insight and take many other things into consideration.

However, I believed in the abilities of my team. We were not victims of our circumstances. Rather, we were brave enough to challenge our realities and strive for a better tomorrow. Despite the emotions that we were going through and the physical and mental struggles that we were dealing with, I declare with pride that we were dedicated to our ambition. I also know that despite our fear and weaknesses, we had unwavering faith in each other. I also knew that no matter what happened, we would not back down until we gave our best.

While I sit here today in isolation, waiting for the inevitable, I look back and thank my stars for the precious moments of companionship which I spent with my loved ones.

Heroes or not, my comrades, brothers and fellow revolutionaries will be my greatest treasures!

6

The Day of the Robbery

"हे आसमां, समय आने दो, हम आप सभी को सूचित करेंगे। फ़िलहाल दिल के अंदर मौजूद लोगों के बारे में हम आपको कुछ नहीं कह सकते।"

(Dear skies, let the time come, we shall inform you all. Currently, we can't tell you anything of those present inside the heart.)

Have you ever felt anxious despite having prepared very well for your goal? How would you feel if you knew that the future of your country depends on you?

A sheer feeling of exhilaration captured my mind and heart!

What we wanted to do was not an easy feat. The Kakori robbery was a dream and we were willing to go to any lengths to make our dream come true.

My comrades and I had been living in very difficult conditions in the past few days. We lacked the conducive environment to nurture our body and mind, but our spirits were undeterred. We were all aware that the robbery was not just the execution of a well-crafted plan. It was going to be a test of our mental agility and physical calibre.

On the fateful day of 9th August, the ten selected members prepared themselves for executing the robbery. Since it was a risky affair, I made sure that we stay on top of things. To make things more structured, we allocated different roles to everyone in the team based on their experience and expertise.

I had narrated the process of execution several times so that the entire team was aware of the whole plan and there were no gaps in knowledge. We had become extra cautious in the last few days so as not to arouse any suspicion towards ourselves. We had stopped meeting publicly to make sure that our presence did not lead to any counterproductive actions.

We had been extremely careful about revealing the exact day of the robbery to people even within the organisation. After all, the HRA comprised of diverse volunteers from across the country. We came from different backgrounds and social status. I know that this robbery was a top priority, and while being completely cognizant of the individual struggles, strengths and limitations of every member, I had to be practical, and therefore, chose the right words with the right people, even within the organisation.

Unlike Congress, we were not being elitist and exclusive. We tried to bring opportunities and space for dialogue without any hierarchal order. But with stakes involved as high as our current situation, we were definitely following a filter to assess who would get to know the details about the operation and who would get to participate. It was done to ensure the safety of not just the members who were participating in the robbery, but also others who were supporting us from the background.

We had very strategically thought of distancing ourselves from those who were already in the public eye. People like Ashfaq, Rajendra Lahiri or Chandra Shekhar Azad had gathered too much attention because of their previous involvement in other operations. So far, they had managed to stay away from the forces to avoid any confrontations. It was their wit, along with their mental and physical strength, that had brought them so far into the revolution. Their insights and inputs in the operation had always been enriching for me as well as others. In fact, they were able to bring nuanced perspectives because of their past experiences that helped us understand what we should be expecting in situations like these.

In case things got out of hand, we had a backup plan – Plan B. This included being a part of different groups that would be stationed in different positions. It also meant boarding different compartments so that if the need arose, either of the two groups could take charge of halting the train. We familiarised ourselves with our weapons so that we were able to defend ourselves if the need arose. Having said that, only those of us who had any experience with guns – including Ashfaq, myself, Azad, Lahiri, Roshan Singh and Rajendra Prasad – would be doing the actual encounter with the forces.

At an individual level, I had tried to focus on my own mental and physical strength to prepare myself for the execution of the robbery. Because even though we were not expecting to go into a hands-on encounter with the forces, I wanted to be ready for all kinds of circumstances.

My growing up years had taught me that physical fitness makes us intellectually alert. It infuses sheer confidence in us, which is needed for stressful situations like this. I encouraged this sentiment amongst my comrades and despite the scarcity of resources, we religiously followed some effective fitness rituals which kept us energetic and motivated.

There were times when I visualised the success of our endeavour. It gave me the courage and strength to manifest our dreams into reality. It also gave me the focus to keep myself dedicated towards the cause. Through the technique of visualisation, I was able to sublimate my fears and apprehensions and feel more calm and composed.

•

The planned day of the robbery finally arrived. We had already split into separate groups. With the help of visual mapping, we had designated our spots.

We reached the Shahjahanpur railway station in the evening. We came to the spot from different directions, not even looking towards each other. As discussed, we got into different compartments. We had concealed our weapons and were dressed in everyday clothes so that nobody noticed us. Strategically, in both the first class and second class compartments, we stationed ourselves right next to the chains that were closest to the exit door so that when we had to pull the chain, we would not have to waste extra time trying to get to the right location. Once the train stopped, getting down would be easier from that point.

Readers, you would be amazed to know that during those times, we did not have advanced ways through which we could communicate with each other. While I was standing in the compartment, I was unable to see the people who were in front of me; I could only imagine where my team members were and hoped that everything was going as per our plan. I wanted to be optimistic and believe that everyone had managed to board the train in the right place and that they had been able to position themselves where they would have prompt access to the chain of the coach as well as to the exit.

We had anticipated that we would meet some British officers in the train. We also noticed that the first class coaches always had members of the British army, so I had told my team members to not lose our calm if we saw some officers around us. We also wanted to be mentally prepared to encounter more guards in the train than we had anticipated.

I held on to my patience to control my inner turmoil and tried to keep calm. In my heart, I was also praying that my comrades were safe. As the train blew its whistle and slowly began heaving out of the station, I closed my eyes and chanted the Gayatri mantra, hoping to harness the blessings of gods and achieve the impossible. At that moment, I was overwhelmed with the love for my country, but I made sure that my emotions became my strength, and not my weakness.

When we were in the train, some of us exchanged subtle looks and shared inconspicuous nods. It was our method of conveying that everything was alright. In my mind, I was trying to reach out to Rajendra Prasad, sending him energy and strength to act appropriately when the time was right.

Without arousing suspicion, I tried to look around to assess the people who were in my coach. I was trying to figure out the level of threat that could come in our way once the operation reached the stage of attack. I kept my eyes and ears open to register every movement that was happening around me.

•

Although it takes a considerable amount of time to reach Kakori from Shahjahanpur, I was so engrossed in the moment, trying my best to stay focussed on everything around me that time just flew by.

Finally, we had reached Kakori. As soon as I saw the signboard which indicated the name of the station, I became proactive. My breath became deeper and my heartbeats became rapid. Despite the screeching sound of the wheels and the melody of the blowing winds, everything had gone silent for me. I had never felt more alive. I closed my eyes to compose myself so that I could embrace what lay ahead of us. The moment, for which I was eagerly waiting, had finally come.

Suddenly, there was a loud noise which stopped the train at the precise location where we wanted it to be. I heaved a huge sigh of relief.

Rajendra had managed to pull the chain of the train.

With my heart pounding against my chest, I opened my eyes. I nodded at my comrades, took out my gun and immediately jumped towards the exit.

"Stay calm. No need to panic. We do not mean any harm to you. We are only here to take back from the government what is rightfully ours. None of you will be harmed if you remain seated."

Similar announcements were being made repeatedly in different coaches of the train. I focused my attention towards the cabin of the guard. I did not know whether people in the other coaches were cooperating or not. I was also paying attention to the sound of any gun fire or walking footsteps. After all, we had anticipated that some of the police guards would definitely come to prevent the robbery.

However, everything had gone as per the plan so far and I was hoping that it would continue to go just as smoothly.

My heart seemed to be rising up in my throat and I could feel that even my comrades were a little nervous. But we managed to keep our calm. It was extremely crucial that we came across as confident and brave. If we sent out a message that we were underprepared, then our plan might backfire.

Followed closely by Ashfaq, Lahiri and a few others, I made my way into the cabin.

"Hands up! Just cooperate with us and you will not be harmed."

I said as I pulled my gun out and faced the guard and the driver.

Unable to respond due to intense fear and shock, they simply looked at our faces which were concealed behind the mask.

"Hand over the chest to us, right now!"

7

Can Something go Wrong?

"न चाहूँ मान दुनिया में, न चाहूँ स्वर्ग को जाना
मुझे वर दे यही माता रहूँ भारत पे दीवाना।"

*(I don't want respect in the world, I don't want to go to heaven.
Give me a boon, mother, to always stay crazy for India.)*

If you are an adult and have experienced even a quarter of your life out in the real world, you will understand this emotion.

If you have ever had a dream, made plans to achieve it or even tried to organise your thoughts in a certain direction, then you know that no matter how hard you try, how well you prepare yourself, how much contingency you think about and how much you mentally prepare yourself for the odds, things are bound to go out of control and you will be thrown off guard. It is not because of lack of collaboration or preparation. It is definitely not because you did not think deep enough or you were not ready enough. But such is the nature of life.

No matter what you plan, how many stories you build in your head about how a certain thing is going to turn out, you will inevitably end up with an encounter that you have no control over. While everything else may not be in your power, the one thing that you can control is your response to stressful events.

When such situations arise, it is critical that instead of being obsessed with what is going wrong, you focus on what can be done right, what is still under your control and how you can make the best of the situation. Otherwise, you will only end up worsening the situation and completely lose out on what could have been a good result.

My dear readers, I know this is easier said than done. Quite frankly, I know I am saying this to comfort myself more than simply giving you an insight. The truth is that despite all our preparations, we lost control of the situation. We came to a stage where we were all shocked to such an extent that we were unable to do anything to salvage it.

We knew the stakes were high and yet, we couldn't think logically in that moment. Of course, now when I think back, I feel that I would have tried to do a few things differently. I would have taken a different approach. However, I knew that something would have definitely gone wrong, given our circumstances. I do not belittle the situation and I do not undermine the gravity of the loss we had incurred, but I do understand that when the stakes are high and when there is so much going on, it helps to be strong. Realistic expectations should be set in our minds so that even when things are going south, we do not mess up so badly that we lose sight of the bigger picture.

The robbery had begun when Lahiri pulled the chain successfully. I had reached the guard's cabin and declared to them to hand over the chest of money while my comrades ensured that nobody approached our coach. It had been planned that we would not let anyone know how many of us were a part of the attack. To accomplish this, we had strategically placed a few people outside the coaches, a little away from the guard's cabin.

Simply because the selected set of people, who had ample experience with guns and were confident enough to portray a strong figure of the attack, were to stand in a cluster near the train. They were supposed to keep shooting in the air every once in a while. This would help create an impression that there were many armed men around the train and that it would be difficult for anybody who tried to approach the guard's cabin to overpower them. This also worked like a cover fire because with the constant firing, nobody would simply walk towards the cabin for the risk of losing their own lives.

As you can see, we had tried to make the plan as fool-proof as possible. This was a well thought-out plan of cover fire. It was the only intended firing that was to happen in the entire robbery. We knew that if the cover firing went on successfully, no policeman would be able to approach us. And if no armed officers were able to approach us, then it was certain that there would be absolutely no need for any firing at anyone from our side. Which is why, we had strictly instructed all the other members of the group to not fire even a single shot. It felt like a smooth plan that could be executed without much trouble.

•

When we started off with our journey, we got to know that there were several police officers on the train. Some British officers were on-board, along with the guard with the chest and the driver. So practically, there had been enough men on the train with enough weapons so they could have easily overthrown us if they wanted to. But as it turned out, none of the officers bothered to even protest or show signs of aggression towards any of us.

When we told them to sit quietly, having clarified that nobody would be harmed and that we only needed to attack the government property, they actually sat quietly. This is an interesting perspective I gained on the men who were in the British forces. If I got to know that any part of my country was under threat, I would have tried my best to deter it from happening. We would not sit down silently and let it all happen in front of our eyes.

But such is the politics of colonial rule! People come and destroy our lives. They take over everything, our land, our freedom, our fields and our treasures. They fly their flags on our soil, rob us of our resources and mark our boundaries as their own.

Of course, they maintain that they are doing everything to make us a more developed nation by giving us modern infrastructure, with railways, post offices and lamp posts. But they cannot fool anyone! The only reason they do this is because they want to sustain their rule and make it more efficient. And even after hijacking our existence, destroying us socially, economically, politically and even psychologically, they still don't consider the country as their own.

The policemen and British officers continued to calmly observe the ongoing operation, just like the other civilians. The guard and the driver hid in whatever corners they could find. Although the government tortured Indians to death to collect the tax they were transporting, there was really no one who wanted to make any efforts to save this money.

Our comrades kept firing regular shots in the air close to the guard's cabin, making sure nobody comes near us. With limited cartridges and bullets, they were being as organised as possible. We could not be weak in our attack even though we didn't have enough weapons. It had to give an impression that it involved large number of heavily armed. This is why they did not fire continuously. They had decided to fire alternatively, at intervals that did not betray the intention.

By this time, I had gotten hold of the chest of money. As soon as Ashfaq saw this, he came up to help me break open the chest. It was heavy chest, so we could not carry it around. We had thought about this long before the operation and knew that every little step would amount to some degree of consequences. If we were to carry the chest around with us, it would mean that our movement would not be agile. It would be difficult to hide the chest from people. Although our escape route has been decided in a way that would keep us away from crowded places, it would still not make sense to carry such a large box with us. During our brainstorming session, Lahiri had also mentioned that we won't be able to dispose of the chest later in a way that the police officers cannot connect it back to us. So, it was a tricky situation. Thus, it was important that we broke it open right there.

Ashfaq was strong and heavily built so he brought a rock to break open the lock quickly. After multiple attempts, he said, "I think the lock is stuck. That's why I am not able to open it. Let me try a different way."

He handed over his gun to Manmath Nath and experimented with his method. While I was looking at Ashfaq with bated breath, hoping that we could crack it soon, something happened which threw us off-guard, changing our lives forever.

•

A couple of coaches away, Ahmed Ali, an unsuspecting civilian had gotten down his coach and was walking towards our cabin. Of course, this was not expected, especially from an Indian!

I looked around closer to see what was happening. Ahmed was really headed towards the women's compartment that was right ahead of him. Ali was travelling with his wife who was seated in the women's compartment. And since the train had stopped for a while, he got down to check on his wife. Clearly, he had no idea about what was going on. He had simply taken this opportunity to walk down to the women's compartment.

It took me a couple of minutes to process this entire information. However, I refocused my attention towards the task at hand, relieved that this was not going to be a risk. But, others were not so quick with their assessment. Manmath Nath was extremely enthusiastic, but he did not have any experience of weaponry. He had barely ever held a gun before and had no experience shooting it. As soon as he saw the man, Manmath marked him as an enemy in his head.

'The man who is walking is no threat to us. We should stay put and make sure not to fire!"

As I was about to communicate this to him, Manmath aimed the gun towards the harmless man in a state of nervousness. I believe he had no intention of shooting him right away. He was just trying to make sure that we were safe. But due to a surge of intense fear and nervousness, he accidentally pulled the trigger and shot.

Amidst the mental chaos, I heard the loud sound of the gunshot echoing through the air. Everything around me froze for that moment.

Ahmed Ali had been hit. He collapsed onto the ground immediately!

•

When I saw the man falling down on the ground in front of me, my first instinct was to rush to him. I wanted to make sure that he got immediate medical attention. But I knew that would be foolish. There was no medical aid around and it would jeopardize the whole operation.

I closed my eyes and calmed my mind, trying desperately to forget what had just happened. Ashfaq, on the other hand, was busy trying to open up the chest, but he did not succeed.

Finally, I picked up an axe and used all my strength to hit hard on the lock. Fortunately, it broke and fell off. Losing no precious time, we took out the money and secured it safely. We had decided to put the entire stash of money into smaller bundles and allocate it into different locations, tied in bed sheets. It was to be distributed to designated people, wrapped up in pieces of clothes we had brought. This way, after the robbery, when we escaped into different locations, we would have some money with us. We were trying to reduce our chances of getting caught.

After securing the money, I signalled for all the other comrades to join me. I checked with everyone to make sure that everything was on track. The money was distributed to the designated people.

For a moment, it seemed we had managed to pull this through. Finally, we had the money in our hands!

The whole operation had not taken more than half an hour. This was just enough time to make sure that we were not rushing anything. But not so long that it would start giving people ideas about stopping the robbery or somehow creating suspicion at the Lucknow station about the delay of the train.

I was rather surprised that we had not been attacked or even stopped by any of the police officers. But I was not going to complain and jinx our good fortune. Silent nods and exchanged looks revealed to me that we were all experiencing a very mixed bag of emotions.

I felt very relieved. But more than anything else, I could sense grief and exhaustion in the eyes of my comrades. I understood that everyone regretted the unintentional killing of an innocent bystander who just happened to be at the wrong place at the wrong time. Deep down, I was also lamenting the death of the civilian. The guilt that I was experiencing was resonating all around me.

"I understand what you all are feeling right now. I know that the death that happened is extremely tragic. But we cannot allow our emotions to overwhelm us, especially at this critical point. Let us not lose focus and finish what we started together. The battle is not over yet!"

Everyone looked at me as I tried to boost the dampened spirits of my friends.

There was no going back now. We had the money in hand, but we still had to escape the location. We had to find our way back to safety and continue to maintain our patience for the upcoming days.

I knew that we were vulnerable, hence, it was extremely important that we stayed focused and positive, no matter what!

8

We must stick to the plan

"ओह, काश हम अपनी मृत्यु से पहले
अपने सपने को सच होते देख पाते।"

*(Oh! I wish we could see our dream
come true before our death.)*

The ten of us were positioned in different parts with different roles and responsibilities. We gave the signal that we had secured the money. It was time to go!

I remember vividly the rush of overwhelming sentiments which I was experiencing at that moment. I wonder if you can imagine our situation and emphasise with us.

We had been in severe debt for the past few months. We had borrowed money to mobilize resources for the revolution. We had reached out to people to donate money for the volunteers, for the resources that we needed. We had to beg for money so that we could print pamphlets and the word could spread fast and make necessary preparations for our publications. We also needed money to travel to different parts of the country, because as you would know, this was no longer a localised affair. We were a nationwide organisation that ran solely through volunteers. Ever since the Congress has taken away their support from us, we barely had any money.

It was not that there were not enough rich Indians around us. And, not that any of these rich Indians were not dedicated to the cause of a free country. It was just that the difference in opinion and the politics of power had become so complicated that it was risky for everyone to align themselves with us. Even those who wanted to support did not want to come out in the open and declare the alliance with us. So, you can understand that holding so much money in our hands after such a long time was a blissful moment.

Most of us had been living in such impoverished conditions that we did not have a nutritious diet for a long time. There had been several days when we had gone through with just a single meal. Surviving on a few morsels, we had spent all of our energy and limited resources in making sure that the HRA survived. We strived to ensure that our volunteers felt some semblance of hope and we were able to provide whatever little amount we could to those who needed it the most in the organisation.

Over the years, we had seen many people reluctantly leave because they did not have a choice. After all, who would be able to function without any money for a long time! Offices had been shut down, positions left abandoned and many operations had to be closed due to the lack of funds. For many months, we had survived on very limited resources for personal use.

I can't remember correctly when was the last time any of us bought a new pair of clothes. I remember all of my friends in torn kurtas and dhotis. They reused the same set of clothes over and over.

Having lived through all that, when I tell you that holding the bundles of money was overwhelming, you can imagine the emotions involved.

•

We had planned for the loot to not be in one place, so it was distributed to the comrades in bed sheets. It would also be easier to hide. Even if a portion of the loot got caught, at least the rest would be secured.

We had distributed the money into smaller pockets, tied them up in pieces of bed sheets and handed them over to people who were to transport them to two different locations. But I hope you understand that this was not the only thing going on in our minds at that moment.

Manmath Nath was struggling to come to terms with the trauma of unintentionally shooting an innocent man. He looked like somebody had shot him; his eyes were swollen and red. I could sense that he had been crying. I could relate with his pain of unintended injuries, whether emotional or physical.

Dear reader, I seem to be repeating myself, but sometimes, the more humane side of the heroes around us remains hidden which prevents them from receiving the sympathy which they deserve. I know Manmath's intentions were pure. I know that his actions were influenced by his nervousness. He had been an active and sincere member of the organisation and always looked out for what was best.

I am not going to deny that he got nervous and agitated very easily. That was one of the reasons why I had kept him close by, to only assist me with the money once we had managed to secure the chest.

After all, I understood his strengths and weaknesses and did not want to pressurise him.

I mean, look at us! Who were we?

Most of us were students; some were young professionals who had just about begun their adult lives. We were passionate and driven for the cause of the country. We had no formal training; nobody had really taught us how to use a gun. We were all stumbling into these lessons on our own in the course of the revolution.

In such a situation, with our faces covered in masks and a rather nervous look in our eyes, we all waited for the last gang to join us. I think everybody had understood that the robbery had cost us a civilian's life. But even in that delicate moment of vulnerability and extreme stress, nobody looked at Manmath with even a hint of accusation. Nobody pointed a finger at him or reprimanded him.

In that moment, we all understood the gravity of the situation and there was an unsaid empathy that resonated with everyone. I am proud to admit that time and again, my friends have inspired me and guided me onto the right path. I thank them from the bottom of my heart for all the inspiration they have provided, either through their actions or their words. The very fact that none of my comrades were angry filled me up with a lot of confidence. It gave me the strength to pull myself together.

This is no secret that I was feeling very vulnerable and emotional. The guilt of having taken an innocent life is not something I could let go of easily. It was the one thing that we had decided on. The robbery was planned against the government property. We wanted to make sure that as an organisation, we bring no harm to fellow countrymen and also to show the government a very categorical and direct attack against their oppression. The death of this man had changed many things about the outcome of this robbery.

I was in deep grief and panic. I was being overwhelmed with a sinking feeling from which I thought I would never recover. But when the ten of us were gathered around the coach with our weapons safely secured, with the bundles of money in our hand, I pulled myself back together for the sake of everyone's confidence.

We knew that we had very little time before the officers broke away from their fearful slumber and started approaching the cabin to assess the loss. Although I was not sure someone could have escaped from the train and rushed to the nearest town, I was still apprehensive. If the word of the robbery had gone out, the police would be reaching for us soon. We did not have any time to waste at this point.

I beckoned all my comrades to come closer and said a few words.

"Today was one of the most difficult days for us. I am very proud of the courage that each of you demonstrated today. We were a great team who stood by each other. What we did today is extraordinary. It will convey to the British government that the fire within us has not died. We are the brave children of our motherland and will fight for her integrity, no matter what!"

As I was talking, Manmath couldn't hold back his tears. I walked up to him and gave him a hug. In that moment, he allowed his emotions to flow, only to begin his journey of healing.

•

After the event, it was important to regroup thoughts and to make sure that we were aligned on what was to be done next. At that moment, my mind was functioning at many levels. There was the whole emotional trauma of the death of Ahmed Ali. Then, there was the nervousness around the robbery and how we had come to a point of no return. But above all this turmoil, there was a very practical and logical approach that we had to follow as per our plan.

Although we had the money in our hands, the robbery was far from over. We had to make sure that we escaped safely as per the plan. The money was hidden securely for the time being, and all members were back to safety. We were mentally and physically prepared for what was coming ahead of us.

The government would not sit in silence after being robbed by a bunch of youngsters. Such an attack was a direct defiance of their rule and posed a questionable threat to their power. If they let this incident slide, they were setting a wrong precedent and making themselves vulnerable to many more attacks. That is why we all understood that the threat was still grave. We would all be under scrutiny by the police for any kind of involvement with this robbery.

We all needed to be extremely cautious about what we did, where we went and who we talked to in the next few days. Any kind of connection could hold us accountable. And it was not just about us. There were many people who were susceptible to being suspected and arrested because of their connections with us. With even one broken or weak link in this entire chain, all of us could be trapped and jailed or severely punished.

Don't get me wrong, I am not scared of the police. And I would not mind being arrested for the love of my country. But there was a lot of work to be done. After all, we were just about to set the revolution into motion. With the success of this robbery, we would be able to mobilise and analyse a lot of our operations in the future.

This was just a very small battle and the war of independence had only just begun.

So it was important for the people around us and for the future of the country that we all stayed focused, confident and sharp.

I called my comrades closer and looked into each one's eyes as we all stood together. I told them that I was proud of them and I told them that this was our first step together towards independence. I told them that they had all managed to play the roles assigned to them successfully and I could not have expected better from them.

I also acknowledged that something unfortunate had happened, without delving deeper into the subject. It could not be changed, but we still had the present and the future in our hands. I told them of the responsibility we held for each other. I reminded them of the integrity that bound us together. I elaborated on the opportunity that waited ahead of us to pay our debt to our beloved motherland.

I told them that this was just the beginning and we had proved our potential in today's test. We were ready for many more such victories.

It seemed to have worked. At least my comrades understood why I was doing this. I saw the smiles of their hearts reaching their eyes and I saw many spirits being lifted as the realisation dawned upon them about what a big step we had all just taken. I reminded them once again about the plan and how they were all supposed to disperse into different locations and continue to act normally in a routine manner so as not to arouse any suspicion.

For just a little while, we wanted to keep the money intact and only release very few notes to make sure we were not catching a lot of attention. Up until this day, we had all been begging for funds, asking everyone for money to sustain our movement. If we suddenly displayed access to so much wealth, we would definitely be raising a lot of eyebrows and giving people something to talk about.

I received nods and encouragement from everyone. Manmath Nath, however, still looked shaken up. I could see that he was trying his best to project himself as strong and confident, but I know that he was failing miserably at it.

I don't blame the guy. What he had just done would be unforgivable in the eyes of god, in the eyes of the nation, and in the eyes of the law. I can't even imagine what he must be going through.

It was not just about the consequences of his action, although that in itself was a matter of grave concern. We had just legally trapped ourselves in a position where we had turned our crime from robbery to manslaughter. This meant that the charges applied towards us would be different and the punishment would be a lot more serious. The fact that a man's life had been claimed would make it easier for the British officers to be ruthless in their approach. It would also make it as difficult as possible for us, legally.

While all of this was running in the back of my mind, I was also thinking about the organisation. I recalled how several people had been against this operation from the beginning. They had warned us severely against the potential violence in the operation. People had also warned us about how not everyone was mentally and physically prepared for this level of stress and, how the involvement of some people more than the others would cause potential risks rather than being a help in the operation.

The most serious implication had been the impression that the organisation and its members had been creating in the country. We had to go to great lengths to make people understand that we were not just young and impatient enthusiasts who wanted to spend our time and energy like an angry mob. That we had consciously and deliberately channelled our efforts towards strategic and political motions. Literature had been our key strength in spreading a message and mobilising the masses.

But this one loss of life in the operation, intentional or not, was going to completely destroy the image that we were trying to create with the Kakori robbery.

We had intended it to be an act of open defiance, but now, it was defiled with violence and death. As much as we would like to celebrate the success of the robbery, we would still not be able to wash our hands of the blood of an innocent man.

I tried my best to comfort Manmatha. I reminded him about the critical role he was going to play in making sure that everybody still held confidence and trust in us. I also told him that I completely understood his intentions and that his heart was in the right place.

I would like to believe that he had felt better because of those words as he gave me a nod. With that, I let him go.

I reached back to the other comrades to make sure that everyone was feeling better. We were still on the right track. We were still going to stick to our plan.

With the share of money in smaller amounts secured in little, inconspicuous pockets, we broke into groups. It was a different set of people than those who had boarded the train. We did not want to be identified as a group or traced by anyone.

We were to split up and avoid main roads and check points. We had to make our way through smaller villages that were lesser on the police grid, to reach our respective homes.

Making sure that no one was alone or vulnerable, we all disappeared into the darkness. We also used different modes of travel to get back to our homes so that no one would suspect our absence. Of course, we had to stay away from trains for the moment. Some of us boarded the local bus while others used bullock carts or even hitch-hiked. We could not risk revealing our identities or even dare to spend any of the money we had gotten from the robbery. It was too soon to have the notes circulated. Instructions were clear to everyone in the group about this. We walked, rode, went our ways, not turning back to even confirm each other's departure with even a nod. We also knew that neither of us had to reach out to the other for a while through any means of communication because several eyes, including those of insiders, would be on us.

As we parted ways to go into different directions, I prayed to all the powers above me to give us all strength and wisdom to continue in the intended direction. We promised to look out for each other and for ourselves in a time that was both extremely critical as well as vulnerable.

9

Hiding from the eyes of the world

"ऐ 'सरयू' यक़ीं रखना, है मेरा सुख़न सच्चा, कहता हूँ, जुबां से जो, अब करके दिखा दूंगा।"

(Dear Saryu, keep your trust, my words are true; whatever I have been saying, I will now turn them true!)

I was back in Shahjahanpur. Comfortable and safe in my location, with a few others. I was maintaining a low profile and going on with routine work, as though nothing had happened. The others had been instructed to do the same. We were all supposed to go back to where we were, without raising much suspicion. None of us were to spend any money immediately or at least definitely not in large amounts as it would cause unnecessary trouble. Everybody knew that we were poor and could not really afford any luxury. This was tricky because we had been living with such limited resources till now. Having money within our reach and still not being able to spend it was really frustrating. But we had to keep the bigger picture in mind.

What I went through during this phase can be broken down into two or three levels – what I was feeling emotionally, what I was bound to do practically and what everything meant to me philosophically.

I will tell you about the practical and logical angle first because that took utmost priority for the safety and security of everything that we had worked for.

The first order of events was to pass on the money to the people we had decided on. We wanted to make sure that the money was sent to the right people at the right time because we could not start disbursing the money too early to draw suspicion. On the other hand, we could not wait for too long because there was a possibility that the police might come, looking for cash. Even if they did not suspect it directly, if such an amount of money was found in our possession, it would link us to the robbery anyway.

Not only would we be arrested, but we would have also lost all the money. We couldn't put so much in jeopardy.

So, as per the original plan, we had already started moving the money to different people in different parts. Some of it was also sent to safe locations and given away as loan so that while we did not have direct possession of money, we would still be able to use it for future requirements.

The second thing to do was to make sure that our daily operations went on as usual so that there was no scope for any suspicion. The ten of us, who had directly participated in the robbery, consciously stayed away from each other. We made sure that no links could be established between us. Before we had left the location of the robbery, we did a quick scan of the periphery to not leave any belongings behind.

Of course we did not have anything luxurious or expensive with us even at that time, but we could not afford to lose whatever little we had, especially the weapons!

Apart from that, there was also the risk of discovery. There was nothing that could be specifically traced back to us, but it would be wise to not leave things to chance. That is why we had instructed everybody to collect whatever possessions they were carrying and to be mindful so as to not leave any trail behind.

Readers, I do not claim any expertise or even experience in these kind of matters; whatever little I know has been based on my observations, discussions and learnings with my comrades. This robbery was the result of brainstorming, ideation and revision of all of these until we thought we had a solid plan at hand.

But I am very cognizant of the fact that there are many things that we did not even know about. In fact, I got to know much later, only during the trial, that there were techniques and perspectives that went way beyond my understanding and knowledge. Our body language, our handwriting and even our expressions could be read and used against us.

I wish I could say now that all of this information would come in handy, the next time we plot something against the government. But alas! I know that in all probability, I will not get a second chance.

•

Back then, I felt like we had done everything to perfection and tried our best to make sure that our plan was impeccable. I only got to know later that we had accidentally left one bed sheet behind due to the chaos and nervousness. I recount now that because of the accidental shot and the unexpected death of Ahmed Ali, Manmath Nath and the people around him had lost composure. This also led the others to lose focus for a while and be involved in trying to take care of the situation. We were not sure what would happen right after the shot was fired.

Were the police officers going to respond by finally waking up to their responsibility and act against us? Was this going to cause uproar in the bystanders who might start protesting or even attacking us? Were our own comrades going to panic or revolt at the sight of a death and therefore disrupt the entire plan?

The uncertainties had been too many and I do not blame anyone for having lost their groove, feeling too overwhelmed to be able to concentrate on the task at hand. But the end result was that we had unfortunately left behind a bed sheet, close to the railway tracks. I can only pin-point this in hindsight because back then, something as trivial as that did not hold my attention. Neither did it present itself as a potential threat to our safety. As funny as it may sound, I wish that as much as I had read about world politics, if only I had paid some attention to criminals, I may have gained deeper insights into their psychology.

When I was focused towards thinking of all the logistics and practical implications about the robbery, I was trying to mentally prepare myself for all the situations. I knew that ever since the unplanned accident happened, the perspective towards the robbery had changed completely. Although we still came out victorious and accomplished the goal of the robbery, both in terms of getting the money as well as disrupting the power play of the government, the implications of the attack changed. Because of the unintended murder, this had become a case of murder and any scope of leniency in the trial had been completely eliminated.

I knew that I needed to prepare myself for the worst. Therefore, I was brushing up on my understanding of the legal framework as well as of all the laws and acts that could be used against us in the trial.

Meanwhile, the emotional turmoil was beginning to take a toll on all of us. Since we had consciously decided to not be in touch with each other for a while, we did not have the luxury to comfort each other, or even get to know about the wellbeing of everyone. There was a sense of grief as well as discomfort in this. Grief, because I understood that my comrades must have been going through the same kind of emotional burden that I was. After all, we had witnessed the murder of an innocent fellow Indian. To add to it, we were forced to pretend as if nothing had happened and continue with our lives without even mentioning anything to anybody.

Sitting here alone in a prison cell, waiting for my last days, I can see that there is great strength in just having someone around to comfort you. Even if you know that your companion cannot really do anything about it, it still helps to know that somebody is standing by your side and understands your perspective. They are there to support you, no matter what!

It was also a discomforting situation because we did not know each other's political stand about what happened. We also did not know whether the episode had pushed anyone on the edge to break us down and turn into an informer. I can't be completely sure whether there was any resentment in anyone's heart and mind against Manmath Nath, but I would like to believe that even if there was, nobody was vocalising it out in the open.

I was in touch with a few people from the organisation who could only bring limited information about the others. More importantly, we were deliberately staying away from getting in touch, so reaching out to each other was only a last resort in case of an emergency.

I must confess that there were letters that were being exchanged through very confidential channels. We used volunteers from unpredictable networks to transmit messages from one person to the other within the organisation and we were still continuing to use those channels for communication. Of course, we used code language and did not mention the robbery or the money directly. But maybe I was too naive to believe that code language would be sufficient to ward off suspicion. I learnt only later that the expertise of the police involved decoding and deciphering such communication on a daily basis.

•

The one person I was most concerned about was Manmath Nath. He was quite vulnerable even before the robbery. We all knew everything about each other's general life conditions as comrades. So, those of us who had nothing to lose could afford to put everything at stake without worrying about the consequences.

However, it is not that simple for those who had responsibilities and obligations. Which is why, when I think of someone like Manmath Nath, I try to place them in a context that made them vulnerable and prevented them from bravely battling against all odds. With all that mental baggage, taking risks and staying focused can be a huge challenge. This is what must have happened with him.

What makes it worse is that after the whole episode was over, I could not properly reach out to him to extend my support and empathy. I could imagine the kind of thoughts that must have been there in his head about the impact of what he had done. I knew that his overbearing guilt was eating him from within. I am sure he realised that all the eyes were on him, and although nobody said anything, he must have still felt the blame for jeopardizing the operation.

To top it all, we had seen political members of the Congress making their observations rather publicly about the incident. Judgments of reprimand were being made and we were being criticized for the violence that happened.

It was almost being portrayed as if this was an intentional move to encourage the youth of the country to take up violence as a means to achieve independence. They thought that we were trying to normalise crime and to make it okay to accept acts of violence against Indians. This was being called as 'revenge against Gandhi' for calling off the non-cooperation movement. And although we had been extremely clear about staying away from violence as much as possible, it was difficult to justify and defend ourselves among those people who were not ready to break away from their prejudiced opinion. This was disappointing, but not completely unexpected!

We knew what the stakes were and I had mentally prepared myself for all kinds of reprimands to come our way, irrespective of what the result and aftermath of the robbery was going to be. What is interesting to note is that while everybody was ready to raise eyebrows, there was hardly anyone who came to demonstrate their support to us.

I noticed that people had consciously began to distance themselves from us so that they would minimise any risk which could come their way if the police caught us.

10

The wave of Revolution

"जिस्म वो क्या जिस्म है, जिसमें न हो खूने-जुनूँ,
क्या लड़े तूफाँ से, जो कश्ती-ए-साहिल में है।
सरफ़रोशी की तमन्ना, अब हमारे दिल में है,
देखना है ज़ोर कितना, बाजु-ए-कातिल में है।"

(What use of a body that's not filled with passion when the times are tough. Our heart desires to sacrifice now; it is time to test the power of the opponent.)

In the last decade, the country has seen a lot of ups and downs in its social, political and economic scenario. We oscillated from being a set of kingdoms and princely states which were building alliance with the British government, to supporting the British in the World War. When we were disappointed from the lack of support on their behalf, we shifted our mode from alliance to non-cooperation. This last decade has been a period of commotion and growth, all at once.

Ever since the first war of independence in 1857, the country's leaders and common masses had finally woken up from their long slumber. The tone of the struggle had changed severely.

As a country, it has taken us a lot of effort to start mobilizing the youth and the common man towards the need for the struggle for independence. And unfortunately, even though that has happened, our approach towards the struggle has been extremely unfocused and irrational.

Some schools of thought have continuously supported Gandhi's principles of non-violence and non-cooperation. Although it has been argued that this was creating a great impression of the political and ethical stand of India in the global picture, the counter argument states that this was more of a propaganda without giving an actionable result, showing concrete steps or a way forward for the revolutionaries to follow.

There were more radical approaches which turned to complete violence and believed in the strengthening of the army against the British Raj.

And then there was us, who believed in a more balanced and hybrid approach in the revolution. We were focused on mobilizing the youth through literature and campaigns, to educate them to understand the nature of the political dynamics in the world as well as in the country, therefore beckoning them to join the revolution in a logical, structured and streamlined fashion.

Before the foundation of the Hindustan Republican Association, the country blindly looked up to the Congress as leaders who would be frontrunners in marching its people towards a free and independent nation. We all looked up to our heroes in the Congress and believed them to be focused enough to take us on the right path.

Gandhi was that iconic figure who held the power to move the nation with a single speech. He asked us to abandon all foreign products during the Swadeshi Movement, and just like that, all of us dropped everything that was British. He asked us to weave our own clothes, write our own books and make our own products. The country followed humbly, despite the many challenges it had to face. He asked us to join the non-cooperation movement with complete Satyagraha and non-violence. We followed that to the best of our abilities, despite being subjected to extreme suppression and exploitation by the British officers.

I wonder if you could imagine us keeping our heads high and our hands tied when children and women were beaten up in front of our eyes, or when the last morsels of food were taken away from our hands, leaving us even more desperate and poor. I wonder if you can place yourself in our shoes and see whether you would have been able to control your anger and not take up the closest available weapon to retaliate, to save a life, or to bring food for your children. Having said that, I do not intend to demean the intentions of the non-cooperation movement. I humbly admit that I was a sincere follower and was deeply inspired by Gandhi's principles of non-violence and truth. I personally mobilized many youngsters to join the movement so that they could channelize their anger and energy into ways that would be productive and inspirational for others to follow.

But I also know the other side of the coin, a little too closely. I know that the country in itself was divided into two sections. These were two different sets of people who enjoyed different social, political and economic situations. One had the privileges of being the elite and rich upper-class Indians. These were sons and daughters of land owners, princes and princesses of the educated class who had travelled around the world and enjoyed the company of the British in whatever capacity they could. These were industrialists, lawyers, doctors or people who lived outside the country now. Their perception of the country and its situation was partially true and was very different from what the major population of the country was experiencing.

Unfortunately, they were also the people who were in positions of power and influence. These were the people who had a major control over the direction of the Indian politics. A lot of them were the eyes and ears of the British officials and were able to influence the policies that were made by the Raj. A big portion of the Congress party belonged to this sector of the population. They were revered by the common masses and enjoyed the position of hero worship.

The Gandhis and the Nehrus had a huge impact on the social, political stand of the country. I have always been in awe with the kind of movement they have been able to create while sitting on discussion panels or simply writing speeches, even if from prison. However, it is unfortunate that the people with so much influence have a very limited and jaded perspective about the country. They were able to understand very little about the struggles of the common man.

If only they could see the challenges and everyday struggles against violence, exploitation, hunger and familial responsibility that turned people towards the so-called violent and unethical means! But they could never identify and empathise with the masses from their elite positions.

This brings me to the other section of the population that makes up the majority of the country. These are people who have very little or no land to their name. These are people who have suffered through generations of poverty and misery. These are people who do not have access to healthcare and education. These are people with minimal skills who have been forced to give up practicing these skills because they are not profitable anymore. Because of colonisation, we have been forced to drop certain lines of work as the market has been killed by the British.

On the other hand, a very specific kind of farming has been forced upon us because that is the only thing that the government would allow to flourish. The poor have gotten poorer and even more desperate. The population is heavily taxed and almost always in debt. There is no food security, job security, no form of insurance against losses, no medical care and barely enough resources to get by. On the contrary, whatever treasures we had in the form of money, gold or any other means, have all been taken away by the British and presented to their beloved queen.

This section of the society has been hungry, scared and suppressed for far too long. So forgive my brazen frustration when I tell you that policies or movements which were proposed while sitting in luxury hotels or fancy conference rooms, did not capture the plight of the poorest of the poor. For someone who was watching his wife or children being beaten up or his infant shrivel away with malnourishment; for someone who had their cattle taken away from them for not being able to repay the debts, it is not easy to commit to notions like non-violence and Satyagraha.

Time and again, dear readers, I have showcased the real and humane elements of the freedom fighters. And I bring it up again so that you are more gentle and empathetic in the way you judge others in the moments of crises.

•

I am writing to you about the post robbery situation of the country. I am happy to inform you that the intended results had begun to show. The amount recovered from the chest was a significant amount. I think it was a total of about eight thousand rupees and it took care of a lot of our challenges.

When we finally started moving the money around, the first thing we did was to pay off loans which we had taken from our well-wishers who had been supporting us. We spent some of the money in acquiring resources that we were going to need in future and also sent money to some of the people so that it would help us with unforeseen expenses. We all experienced great relief and pride because this was not a personal gain. This was something that benefited the entire organisation. It also helped us to repay all those who had stood by us and shown faith in us.

At the same time, because of the resources available to us, the impact that something like this would create on the entire country was incomparable. It brought overwhelming gratitude in the lives of those of us who had been in debt for too long or who were not able to afford even a square meal for quite a long time now. And this, as you can understand, was the most immediate and prominent effect that we saw, at a micro level.

Although I can appreciate that this might not mean a lot to you as a distant observer, this little victory is what helped us to regain our confidence and build enough physical and mental strength, to continue with the struggle that lay ahead of us.

•

The more prominent result of the robbery was the impact that it created on the nation. As soon as word got out that a full-fledged attack had been successful on a train in Uttar Pradesh, one of the first things that were inquired into was the intention of the robbery and the result. When people began to learn that this was an attack by a very small number of people and directed specifically towards the tax money which was the only loot that was taken away from the train, they were impressed by our courage.

One of the major reasons for conducting the robbery, if you remember, was to create a sensation in the country through open defiance of the authority of the British government. We wanted to send a strong message that we were not going to sit quietly and watch while our own money and resources were being stolen. The number of letters and pamphlets that were circulated after the robbery was a strong message to let us know that the country had heard our calling and received it well. So many articles in the media were portraying us as heroes. In the following weeks, many young men and women reached out to the Hindustan Republican Association, volunteering to join the revolution and contribute in every possible way. Our poetry and literature was circulated vigorously amongst the masses.

The Kakori robbery was not looked upon as a petty theft or a crime of violence. Instead, it was being perceived as an event that had set the motion of revolution into a gigantic wave. More and more people of India were willing to participate in the revolution. I was delighted to see that young and educated youth were getting motivated to write and publish more to create an awareness that would help us in the long run. Our fear that the robbery should not propagate crime was washed away, as the youth was being driven towards actionable inputs and strategic collaboration to make sure that we were ethical, responsible and politically enlightened.

•

Dear reader, I hope you can understand the gravity of what had happened and are able to appreciate the relief and pride that I was feeling. I am sure my comrades were feeling the same way as we all sat isolated in our prisons. We had the comfort to know that the operation, for which we are ready to give up our life, had been like a shooting star and was creating ripples in the ocean. This had been a dream for far too long. With teary eyes, I write that I feel humbled and elated.

I don't want to just blow my own trumpet by telling you what heroes we had become. I also take complete responsibility for the stress and misery that had been caused to my comrades and their friends and families. Never before had the government been attacked so brazenly! I know it is not a trivial matter, but ten youngsters with barely any experience with weapons, with hardly a penny to their names, who were considered naive individuals and ignorant fighters among other things, had been able to rob a train. That too, near a very prominent location under the British Raj.

We had literally opened a chest full of money and sent out a strong message that the money belongs to the people. Even the commotion of the revolution that the aftermath had caused was a huge slap in the face of the government.

I don't mean to sound arrogant, but on behalf of all of us, I am very proud to say that for the first time, we gave the government what they truly deserved, by rubbing their noses in the very soil that they hated so much. Having said that, I know that we had poked the lion in its den and angered the beast. The robbery had been such a bold act of defiance that it completely shook up the centre.

•

Ever since the Rowlatt Act, the British officers had become complacent because they were confident about the unshakable oppression with which they had managed to curb all kinds of civil unrest and petty crimes. This robbery came as a loud explosion in the silence of the night. It was insulting and infuriating for them to know that we had been able to overpower the authority. They were also acutely aware of the fact that once such an operation had been publicized as successful, the population would grow even more impatient with the suppression and more such events would start happening all over the country. They were under a lot of pressure to nip this in the bud and were definitely set to go the extra mile to make sure that all perpetrators of the operation were punished. They wanted to set an example for the population to understand that the British government would not be undermined and such actions would not go unpunished.

We could hear the news of interrogation and investigation all around us. We even knew that several eyes were on us. People were waiting for the slightest mistake from our end, or the smallest discovery to trace the origin or even the most distant link to the robbery.

We were in an extremely precarious situation, mostly alone and isolated from one another. We were holding on with our hope, waiting for the storm to either settle down or to blow us away.

11

Introspection within the prison walls

"यदि देशहित में मरना पड़े मुझे सहस्त्रों बार भी, तो भी न मैं इस कष्ट को निज ध्यान में लाऊँ कभी। हे ईश! भारतवर्ष में शत् बार मेरा जन्म हो, कारण सदा ही मृत्यु का देशोपकारक कर्म हो।"

(If I have to die for the country, even a thousand times, I will not even consider it as trouble. Oh god! I wish to be born a hundred times in India and to die each time for the benefit of the country.)

The storm was definitely on the rise and I could hear the sound of damages in its wake, all around me. I could see that the police had started looking out for the smallest signs of suspicion. I was also getting information from other people stuck in a similar situation. Everywhere I went, I felt like I had eyes on me. I was trying my best to keep a watch on the developments around me, but I had to be careful.

I knew that police investigations had begun at a deeper level and they were looking for connections with the organisation, so that they could associate our involvement with the Kakori robbery. I also got to know that my whereabouts at the time of the robbery were being inquired into and it was being noted when I left the town and when I got back.

Some of my well-wishers, who were also helping out as informants, would keep an eye out and be in contact with the police officers to get inside information. I also met influential people in Shahjahanpur at that time. It always felt like the government would not be able to touch me.

In fact, some police officers had even come to enquire about some details in relation to the Kakori robbery from me directly. Interestingly, even at that time, I did not feel threatened or scared. I was so sure about our plan and how well we had executed everything that I was confident that the police would not be able to arrest me. Even if they did, they would not find any proof to hold me back.

In retrospect, it feels like I was being too arrogant or perhaps too naive.

I did not understand the expertise of the police investigators and how they would certainly observe little things and begin to establish links of one person with another, of one event with another.

While I was connected to a very small network of people in Shahjahanpur and was able to get some inputs from them, it was not sufficient information to understand the actual progress of the case. We only got to know about it in bits and pieces when the police officers visited somebody or were asking questions about somebody. But apart from that, we were clueless.

Looking back, I realise how extremely under-prepared we had been at that time. The truth is that the robbery had not been a fool-proof plan. I don't say this because the execution was an issue; in fact, the execution was one thing that went on better than imagined. And I say this notwithstanding the fact that we lost an innocent life in the heist.

Please don't get me wrong, I am not trivialising the loss of that life and still carry the guilt of Ahmed Ali's death. But please forgive me when I am willing to overlook this one loss over the gain of several years of hard work and accomplishment that would go a long way in propelling the revolution.

I know that all deaths are glorified as martyrdom. It is a very political and strategic way of easing the conscience. Despite all that, it was true that as much as this was unavoidable, and as much as it pains me to relive that moment when Manmath Nath shot Ahmed Ali, I replay the entire situation in a way that this would not have happened had I been able to respond sooner. I hope I was able to sensitize my men that the stranger walking towards us meant no threat at the precise moment. But I know that this is a futile exercise, and no matter what I do, I cannot take back the loss.

I also know that if I keep repeating and re-emphasising on that one point again and again, I will be creating a sense of fear, discomfort and lack of confidence among the people who have already been feeling extremely guilty about the mishap. By calling out that one mistake repeatedly, I will not only be increasing their burden, but also judging them in an unfair manner. Nothing can replace a life lost, but I also understand the context and the situation in which this happened.

So forgive me if I hold my sympathies out for the men who are now ready to give up their lives. Forgive me if I am open to crediting this death to martyrdom for the larger cause of our freedom. Forgive me if I try to diffuse the entire situation to ensure that the confidence within the organisation that is already headed towards shambles may be preserved in some form.

•

–: *Kakori* :–

The situation of the Hindustan Republican Association needs no reminder. Up until the success of the robbery, we had been in severe debt, incurred several losses of lives and resources each day. We were losing volunteers due to the lack of funds and offices had been shut down. This was coming at a huge cost for all of us. The momentum, that had taken months and years of hard work to build up, was slowly coming down under pressure. People were beginning to give up and we could not force them as this was an organisation based on volunteering.

The Kakori robbery, however, had put us back on the map of success and had become a huge buzz all over the country. We had angered the government and triggered them to respond provocatively and violently. The whole country was watching the atrocities on the innocent. Even before the attack, undignified conduct by the police was a commonplace affair. But once the Kakori robbery had become famous, the British government had no option but to save their face by retaliating in the best way they could.

Friends and families of the suspects, unfortunately, suffered a lot in this process. They were arrested, tortured, interrogated and followed relentlessly and mercilessly. Intimidation in itself would have been sufficient to break the spirit of many. But what made things worse was that the organisation itself had been hollowing up from inside, even before the Kakori robbery had happened.

An organisation basically starts with a philosophy or a vision in the form of an objective that is envisaged by a person or a group of people who have a like-minded approach, who believe in the same accomplishments and who are aligned towards both the cause as well as the journey that leads up to it. This collective approach helps to build a strong foundation of an organisation. As this body begins to show positive growth and establishes itself as progressing on the right path towards its intended goals, the organisation begins to establish credibility among other people, therefore drawing attention that is lucrative for its expansion.

This often leads to funding as more and more people are convinced about the vision. But more importantly, it leads to growth by involving many different people who align themselves with the idea of the organisation and want to contribute in some way for mutual benefit. This is typically how a systemic progress of an organisation works.

However,with growth comes intensive responsibility and uncontrolled diversity. Although we do believe that diversity is a healthy reflection of inclusivity, unfortunately, it may also lead to the weakening of the principles on which the foundation of the organisation was placed. Philosophies begin to dilute and approaches begin to metamorphose into forms that differ from the original intent.

I would like to point out that it is not necessary that there are always ill intentions or poor motives behind this, but because of the involvement of many people with different schools of thoughts and ideas, there are bound to be some counter-productive results. This is exactly what was happening in the HRA as well.

As more and more people joined the organisation, different elements of power and dynamics, politics and strategies started shaping up. Sometimes too much enthusiasm and vigour can be misrepresented to the larger audience. This leads to a difference in power dynamics and can cause emotions as extreme as hatred for our own comrades.

I had begun to see signs of this amidst some sections of our organisation. Principally, we had strongly endorsed that there would be no hierarchy in the organisation and everybody would have direct access to me, considering that I was the central axis of the HRA. However, unintentional positions of hierarchy had started developing and some people had started assuming roles of being the leaders among their group members.

Unfortunately, simple instances of difference of opinion had begun growing into discontent and even passive aggression. When this issue was brought to my notice, I called all the involved members and gave them a sound scolding, reminding them of the cause for which we have all come together and what is at stake. I also reminded them of the responsibility that they carry because of the position they hold. I told them about how not only the entire organisation, but the entire country is looking up to us. How young individuals find inspiration in guidance in everything that we say or do.

I reminded them of the very delicate situation that they were in and how their words and their actions will not only reflect the fabric of the organisation, but also help to create and endorse a culture of integrity and togetherness for the future generations.

I hoped that such discussions had helped to diffuse the situation and instilled the sense of integrity that we all desperately needed to carry on with. I could see that such interactions helped people to regroup their thoughts and re-orient themselves with the spirit of fellowship and team work.

I only realise now that even though I tried hard and the intentions of my comrades were pure, a difference of opinion at the root had been created and subconscious distancing has started happening within the organisation. This became one of the reasons for the downfall of HRA, along with the betrayal that led to the arrest of many from the organisation.

It is because of this distancing and ultimate betrayal that I am sitting here in this miserable prison cell, thinking about all the mistakes that I have made; all the judgments that I was wrong about and all the things that I should have thought and seen differently.

The distance that had been created within the organisation was not only being counterproductive to our operations, it was also creating opportunities of mistrust and lack of confidence within the groups. Some close comrades had warned me about what they were foreseeing, but I think I was a little too drunk with confidence, and so focused on looking at the bigger picture that I couldn't see it coming.

After all, I held the most important position in the organisation and I was its founder. I think it is because of this I was immune to looking at its faults, just like a proud parent sees their child as the brightest star in the sky. Now I realise that there were many mistakes that I had made and I could have done better by preparing myself better if I really wanted to run an organisation at such a big scale and with such a high impact.

•

You remember, I had mentioned that one of us had left a bed sheet behind by mistake. At that time, I had not thought too much of it because it was just an ordinary piece of cloth that had ended up being thrown by the side of the track and it could happen with anybody.

However, now I am stunned to see the capacity and extent to which investigations can probe into cases. An expert team of investigators from Lucknow who had visited the spot of the robbery had done a very intensive search around the perimeter and had discovered the bed sheet conspicuously thrown near the tracks. They had collected it as evidence. Unfortunately, this has become an important lead for them.

I found out later that the bed sheet had a stamp of a washerman in Shahjahanpur. This allowed for the police to guess that at least some of the parties involved in the robbery were in some way connected to the town. This led them to extending their investigations into my city. They managed to locate the washer man and trace the bed sheet back to one of the persons who was closely connected to one of the members of the HRA. These gentlemen had already been on the radar of the police for quite some time and it did not take them long to establish the link of his involvement in the robbery.

Can you imagine how such a small and careless mistake could have led to such a critical development in the case for the investigating officers!

However, as I found out later, with a deeper understanding of the law, such a discovery could have eventually been dismissed as circumstantial evidence if we had known how to run the case in the right manner. But, we were too naive to understand that point about what should be said and done!

More importantly, it was not just this discovery that got us in. Unfortunately, we had a snake living amongst us as our own. He was a very close friend of someone I trusted blindly in the organisation and therefore never questioned his integrity. I got to know much later that this one man was the singular reason for the downfall of not just the members of the Kakori robbery team, but also the organisation as a whole.

I was shocked and betrayed, but also extremely humbled in the realisation of my mistakes because people had warned me that I trusted people too much too soon. Although nobody could have predicted that he would betray us, I guess it was my carelessness of not screening people well enough who became a part of the organisation. It was this letting people in without proper background checks and interrogations that led to this one man revealing all of our secrets and plans. He told the police about the Kakori plan, and gave them enough evidence and details to cause irreparable damage to the organisation.

It was because of him that many of us eventually got arrested and many of our operations were caught even before they could be executed. The HRA shrivelled down to nothing more than a name of a group of people who could have been successful.

I still have not managed to understand what we could have done so wrong to force him to betray us in this manner. To give up on us with such vengeance that it destroyed everything. If I could, I would go back in time and reach out to him to understand why this happened. If there was any way to revise history, I would not want to reprimand him or take revenge for what he had done. Instead, I would like to understand his point of view, and as I have so humbly learnt now, to assess my own mistakes that must have led to such actions on his part.

I don't know if I am comfortable enough to sympathize with him for what he did because this was not just personal loss. It was unfair and cost us our lives and the future that we had dreamed for our country. It was because of him that I will not be alive to witness the sun rising in my free country, so it is not going to be easy for me to forgive him. But from where I am right now, I see the futility of vengeance. A part of me really wants to reach out to him to know what really happened.

I have no qualms in admitting that he was not the only one who surprised me. There were many other members of the organisation, who unfortunately turned into informers of the police and gave statements against us in the court of trial. I cannot be completely sure as to why this happened, but I know they were all scared and had their own reasons. Some of these men were weak-spirited and therefore it comes as no surprise that they succumbed to the police pressure. But there were some others whose betrayals hit me harder than I had thought.

Unfortunately, there is nothing I can do about it now and these realisations will do me no good in this life. But dear readers, I do hope that if my writings reach you, then it helps you to provide at least some kind of insight into understanding human psychology.

•

Banwari Lal Bhargava was a part of the HRA and also a participant in the Kakori robbery by way of sourcing weapons. He became the approver in the subsequent court case to evade capital punishment and for monetary support extended by the government.

Ram Prasad Bismil expressed unwillingness in mentioning Banwari Lal's name in his autobiography as he could foresee grave consequences for the 'fellow comrade' and his family if this knowledge became public.

12

Betrayed by our very own

"किसी को घृणा तथा उपेक्षा की दृष्टि से न देखा जाए, किन्तु सबके साथ करुणा सहित प्रेमभाव का बर्ताव किया जाए।"

(Don't look at anyone with hatred or reprimand. Everyone should be treated with kindness and love.)

It is said that when things have to go wrong, you contribute to it with your own mistakes and stupidity. A third person watching from a distance would be able to tell that you are headed for danger. But you would be so engrossed in the situation at a micro level that you would fail to notice all the traps and holes that have been dug up around you. In fact, you may unintentionally have dug a few of those holes without realising. In such cases, I wonder if having an outsider's perspective would help.

Now, I understand my own weaknesses and all the places where I had been wrong. Iam able to pinpoint the exact places where I could have taken a better decision. I know that if I had a chance to do it differently, we would not be in this situation. We would have gotten away with the Kakori robbery as a successful accomplishment.

None of my comrades or I would be in jail and I definitely would not have had a death sentence. I think it is just a matter of perspective, introspection and retrospection to understand about self and the situation around us in a manner that we could not have even imagined back then.

As you would know, dear reader, I am an avid reader and writer. It is no surprise that I am spending the last days of my life writing and trying to recall all of my experiences that could perhaps be a representation of our collective knowledge.

Have you ever read a book twice? Could you see the hidden messages in it which you may have missed the first time? What is going on in a person's mind when they are expressing their thoughts and experiences comes in many layers. The deeper we delve into them, the more we realise the significance of each word. This is true for life, just as it is true for literature.

When we are in the eye of a storm, we are generally only able to see what is right ahead of us. Very often, our mind is engrossed in what is behind us, but foresightedness is when we are able to broaden our horizons and look beyond the immediate. That enables us to understand and assess the situation better. I wish I had this perspective back when I had control, and had been able to see what was going on. I wish I had listened to different people, been more open to their opinion.

We did all the planning on our own, thinking of ways in which we could be harmed and countering it with a plan. We thought we had it all figured, but now that I think about it, I can think of a lot of people who I could have reached out to for guidance.

Despite the difference in opinion, I did revere and respect so many leaders of the Congress. We were connected through the same cause for the country and I could have reached out. Honestly, I don't know what the end of this revolution will be like and I don't understand which path will take us to win the independence of my beloved nation. But I do know that I could have been a part of that.

I could have been alive and strong enough to witness a free country. I don't know if you can feel my longing, but it is as sharp as a dagger digging into my heart. I feel regret for missing out on things that could have helped me carve a different future.

•

The aftermath of the Kakori robbery had so many different levels that it was hard to keep up. More protests and awareness had spread through the country.

I got to know that Bhagat Singh, who I adore and revere, had been writing extensively about the robbery and has been spreading the word along with Chandra Shekhar Azad and others. I see that people were working very hard to spread the word across and were gaining support from all sides. I wish that some of the support had reached me.

As you would know, right after the robbery, the police had become extremely meticulous and active towards anyone who could be remotely involved in the incident. Despite our caution, some of the notes circulated after the robbery had managed to reach Shahjahanpur and this was making it easier for the police to establish a link between the theft and the people involved.

Some of my friends and well-wishers had reached out to me with news from very reliable sources that the police were almost certain about my involvement. I got to know that my arrest was imminent and it could be happening any moment.

When I think back now, I can only blame it on my ignorance that I did not take their words seriously. I was confident that the police were actually not able to trace the connections back to me. I believed for some reason that I would not be arrested.

Even more arrogant, I believed that even if they did, they wouldn't be able to detain me since they would have no evidence to establish any proof of my involvement and therefore not be able to convict me with any charges. It is nice to have faith, to have confidence and to believe that things are going as per plan, and that the pillars on which the foundation of your thoughts and actions are based are sorted and will continue to hold with the strength that you intend it to be.

But that does not always work, does it? As I would get to know later, the very faith the I carried for the people around me became the reason for my downfall. The betrayal of those closest to me has led to the arrest of all of our team members and will most likely cause our deaths.

Despite several warnings of my imminent arrest from well-wishers around me, I was no longer trying to escapc from Shahjahanpur. On the contrary, I continued to go about business as usual, meeting with other people, carrying on with my business and following the daily routine. On one such evening, I had gone out to visit my friends, where again I was informed about people closing in and there being a potential threat of my arrest anytime soon.

While I heard them out respectfully, I paid no heed to their warning. Now that I think back to that time, quite frankly, I was beginning to get tired and bored of all the hiding and waiting. There was so much to be done, so much to plan and so much to execute, and we were forced into anonymous existence, away from each other, living in isolation and losing precious time.

•

If I'm being completely honest with you, I also wanted to test the strength and integrity of my country and to assess their forbearing and reaction in a situation like this. A whole bunch of us had done whatever it took to make sure that the revolution was able to head strongly towards its intended goal.

So I wanted to understand whether the country would really care about people like me, people who were nobody, who did not have any power and did not come from the background of royalty or a lot of influence. I know when the stalwarts of the countries are jailed, the whole world comes down to their feet and treats them like god. They are given all the privileges of the world and are able to control all the activities that go on outside from within the prison walls.

But most of us came from humble beginnings and did not have the kind of backing that my privileged counterparts did. I think I wanted to test the waters and see what kind of impact our actions are creating in the hearts and minds of the people who we are willing to give up our lives for. The revolutionaries and freedom fighters who had come before me narrated their experiences of prison. It had sounded like a life-transforming experience and of course there was an honour in being arrested while fighting for the country.

I am not trying to glorify the prison or its experiences, because I am going through that right now and it is not even remotely close to being comfortable. But I did want to experience that side of life and I did want to understand the sentiments that people go through behind bars – noble, respected people who have done great things and have been arrested for the cause of the motherland.

I think it was a mix of all these feelings that led me to become careless and slow towards keeping caution.

And the results showed themselves really quickly. On the way back from visiting my friends close to my house, I saw a policeman paying very close attention to me. It was rather surprising because it was late in the night and that kind of patrolling was not common in my area. But even then, I did not think much of it and returned to my house without giving it a second thought.

However, around 4 in the morning, I was woken up to the loud banging of something strong being punched against my door. Several policemen were using the end of their guns to bang open the door.

Still deep in my sleep, I opened the door and asked them what the matter was. The policemen were polite in both their body language and their language. They asked me if there was anything objectionable or illicit in the house. I replied that there wasn't. Mind you, I was under the impression that this was going to be an interrogation or search and then they would leave!

A policeman searched the house thoroughly and found some letters in my coat pocket. These were the letters that I was supposed to post the previous evening, but since the postman had already left for the day, I decided to keep them back with myself and go to the post office again in the morning. They scanned through the letters and found one of them to contain objectionable content that could be used against the British government.

I had completely forgotten that it had been a letter to some of my associates. Although still not in direct language, it was enough to imply that something was brewing against the government. The policeman also asked me if I had any concealed weapons, which I did not. After this, they respectfully requested me to come with them to the police station immediately.

I just had a piece of cloth wrapped around my waist. They did not even let me change and I was asked to leave with them in that one piece of cloth early that fateful morning. Thus, the bubble of my illusion was broken and I got to know about the many flaws and issues that had been brewing in my own organisation that had come back to me with such vengeance.

•

During the conversation with one of the policemen back at the police station, I was told about a few plans and some key activities that only one other person in the entire organisation knew about. When I first heard the policeman say those things, I went into a state of shock. I could not believe that something like this had really happened.

I had trusted this man like a treasure and valued him as a key member of the organisation. To hear those words come from the policeman, I became certain beyond doubt that this person had turned into an informer and betrayed the organisation by revealing some extremely critical information to the police. I do not wish to reveal the name of this man, although it is difficult for me to hold any kind of sympathy or moral obligation towards him. I don't know what I had done to him for him to stoop to this level. But in that moment, I was certain that I was doomed and that this arrest was no more an instance to be taken lightly.

Within the next few days, I got to know that several other arrests had been made across the state and a total of forty people from the organisation had been arrested for direct or indirect involvement with the Kakori robbery.

This included my beloved Ashfaq, Roshan Singh, Rajendra Lahiri, Banarsi Lal and several others. From what I understood and gathered, Chandra Shekhar Azad and a couple of other fortunate people had managed to escape arrest.

But the rest of us were all being held captive and were in different parts of the state. Interestingly, all the prisoners were kept in isolation. Later, I understood that they wanted to create a degree of confusion by not letting us meet each other. We had no way of knowing what the other person had revealed or admitted to. In the next week or so, about seventeen of our men had to be released because there was not enough evidence against them.

I realised that there was information that the one man who I had trusted the most did not have. Since he could not provide any information regarding that matter, the other people had to be let go. This confirmed my doubt; I was able to place all the facts together to understand how much she had known and how much he would have been able to reveal to the police.

•

For the next several days, different policemen came to us and talked to us about many different things. They would never directly question us about the robbery, but ask indirectly about our family. Things about what we did, to maybe trap us in our own words without being the obvious villain.

I was spellbound by the tactics and could imagine the kind of impact it would be having on some of the members who had been arrested.

I got to know that we had been charged with not just robbery, but manslaughter. Ashfaq and a few others had also been charged for involvement in another case before the robbery.

Overall, because of the information gathered and because of the secrets revealed by the informer, we were stuck in a very serious situation. This was not going to be easy!

13

A web of legal processes

"मिट गया जब मिटने वाला फिर सलाम आया तो क्या!
दिल की बर्बादी के बाद उनका पयाम आया तो क्या!"

*"What is the use of the greeting when someone has passed away?
What's the use of those messages, when the messenger bought it after hope died?"*

The investigations were getting intense and different sections of the police forces had come to visit us to establish our involvement in the robbery as well as in other activities against the government.

I was getting more and more confident that all the people who held key positions in the organisation were behind bars and the entire network was crashing right in front of our eyes.

What happened over the next few weeks and perhaps months was nothing short of an ordeal. Different tests were designed through crafty means. People would come disguised as well-wishers and discuss with us about the probabilities of the verdict in case we were able to provide any useful information to the government. They tried to bribe us, threaten us and move us with their words and promises.

Unfortunately, we were all imprisoned in isolation and did not even have access to each other directly so that we could understand what was going on. The documents and letters that were recovered were analysed by handwriting experts; the weapons that were found were also analysed.

Many of our resources and information were discovered. The superintendent of police would pay regular visits, talking to us about different kinds of consequences and thereby trying to manipulate the already vulnerable state that we were in.I would be a fool if I were to claim that I was not scared. I hope you understand that fear was acting in many different forms now.

Too much was left for our imagination and that became the greatest source of fear. When some of my friends tried to send us a lawyer, I tried my best to secure some help for those of us who were at a greater chance of breaking down. Long before the arrest, some of my friends had warned me that our dear friend Banarasi Lal was a weak link and posed a huge threat for the operation.

I can understand that his intentions were not wrong, but it was quite obvious that he was a nervous fellow and vulnerable to pressure. I had spoken to a lawyer and even tried to convince him to speak to Banarasi Lal and to provide him with some kind of confidence to support and enlighten him about the situation that we were in. I was hoping that this conversation and support provided to him would at least give him some strength and patience and perhaps prevent him from breaking down when the police approached him.

However, when things have to go wrong, people even in their sound minds start going in the opposite direction and stop paying heed to important and useful insights. I myself have done this in the past, so I can imagine it happening to other people as well. I don't hold it against them.

Our lawyer did not pay heed to my warning. He did not take up the matter with the urgency that it deserved. And just as I had predicted, the police got to Banarasi Lal the day before the lawyer could even contact him. They kept him in isolation, gave him a lot of psychological pressure and threatened him in several ways. They even bribed him with the promise that if he turned into an informer, the final decision would definitely go in his favour and he would not have to be worried about any kind of punishment around his involvement in the robbery or the organisation. I know that Banarasi Lal had his own set of responsibilities and all this while, not being able to come in contact with others must have put him in a vulnerable state of mind.

•

When you have people who you can trust, who can understand and empathize with you, your mind has the power to overcome the most unthinkable of obstacles. Banarasi Lal had been in isolation and must have thought about the worst consequences.

I am certain that he did not wish any ill to come upon us intentionally, but he was scared to death because of his own mind games and perhaps all the pressure that the police must have created on him. They must have made him visualise the consequences that were to fall upon the rest of us, and what would happen if he did not cooperate with them. It must have made him feel that he had no other choice. They bribed him and forced him into a corner by placing him in a situation where he had to choose between his own life and the life of those who had been brothers in arms.

I understand why and how he must have turned into an informer and talked to the British officers, revealing all of our secrets.

I got to know later that even Banarasi Lal did not reveal more than just the necessary details that would get him out of punishment. I will go to my grave without any grudges or qualms against this man, because despite his vulnerable situation and the intense pressure that he was in, he still refused to recognise us during the trial. In his way, he did the best he could to help us, while still saving his own life.

I remember the guilt and apology in his eyes during the trial, but there was still pride and determined confidence in his defiance in knowing that the British officers had not completely broken him down. Whatever little power he had, he used against them in the fact that he denied to recognise us as the participants of the robbery.

•

Unfortunately, the damage had already been done by the betrayer earlier, the person who I am deliberately not naming because I fear that anger and defamation that this will bestow upon him might even reach his friends and family. I don't want his generations to come to bear the brunt of his betrayal.

You may think of it as a matter of redemption for me, but I do not seek vengeance on those who have done wrong to me. I ask the almighty for forgiveness and blessings even for those who refused to help us in our most desperate times.

During the trial, I found out that the legal framework was more like a web of traps spread by the British government.

While I was trying to understand the legalities that were involved in this case, we were also trying to reach out to people in Lucknow and Banaras to help us find a good lawyer to lead our case.

A very crafty step taken by the law was to assign a public prosecutor to our case, who we knew for a fact was against me.

There was this lawyer called Jagat Narayan Mulla, who held a strong and irreparable grudge against me. He was assigned as a public prosecutor for our case. And the mention of his very name made it extremely clear to us about the intention of the government.

We understood that they had no intent of giving us a fair trial and definitely set out to make sure that our efforts in the process were diffused or at least stopped in whatever way they could, while still staying within the legal boundary. The chances of us not finding even a decent prosecutor to defend our case was too high, and therefore, I would have to try my best to make sure that I at least understood the situation that we were getting into.

Those of us who had been arrested in the Kakori robbery were technically supposed to be political prisoners. This meant that we had certain rights and access to certain resources like books or conversations with people. We should have been allowed to write letters and have access to media and publications.

However, the British government had been so poisoned by our brazen attack that they were trying their best to keep us away from these privileges. They had imprisoned us as common prisoners as though we had committed petty crimes and they were making sure to deprive us of any privileges and resources that we otherwise were entitled to.

•

With whatever little we had under control at that time, we tried to draw inspiration from the people who had come before us. Gandhi had always been a staunch supporter of non-violent means of creating a movement; he felt that this was one of the strongest ways to send a message to the world that you are in the right and that your actions and your revolutions come from the right place. Such actions speak of ethics and a moral background, and are known to have a deep impact, even in world politics. Inspired by his thoughts, we decided to do the same in prison.

All of us decided to go on a hunger strike in protest of not being treated as political prisoners. This strike went on for various days for different members. Since we were not kept together, we did not know for sure what was going on in the other locations. But despite that, we tried our best to maintain uniformity in our approach.

I think back to my time in prison, when we were all on strike. I am filled with a certain sense of pride and joy. This was a time when we would sing songs for the love of our country and try to raise others' spirits and confidence. It was also the time where I wrote many poems and letters for the world. I poured my heart out to express my emotions and my love. I also wrote about the very human emotions that we were all going through during the time of struggle.

•

I remember that one time during Basant Panchami when those of us who had access to each other and had managed to get some goodwill from the police officers, collectively wrote a song called *Mera rang de basanti chola* and sang it with our spirits high and our eyes wet with love and joy. I know this sound like a romanticized version of the struggle, but little joys like these can go a long way in the state of desperation and misery we were experiencing. Despite all the struggles and all the battles, the manipulations and the betrayals, it still feels like an honour to have had the opportunity to contribute even in the little way to ignite the fire of revolution.

Even outside the walls of the prison, there were many people who were showing their support and joining in on the protest from outside. With everybody's eyes on the trial, several leaders of the country – including Motilal Nehru, Madan Mohan Malaviya, Muhammad Ali Jinnah, Lala Lajpat Rai, Jawaharlal Nehru, Ganesh Shankar Vidyarthi, Shiv Prasad

Gupta, Shri Prakash and Acharya Narendra Dev – all came to our support and expressed their vehement protest against the way we were being treated in the prison.

Despite many petitions, we were not given fair representation in the court, which is why I had decided that I would fight my own case and was trying to get as much legal counsel as possible.

I express my gratitude to the people who went out of their way to show their support for us. Eventually, legal defence was provided by the likes of Govind Vallabh Pant and Mohanlal Saxena. I still remember when I had gone into court, the judge had been surprised to hear me speak such fluent English and that I understood the legal framework with such depth. In fact, he expressed his surprise and appreciation as well. I had made it a point to let him know that we Indians could not be taken lightly, and it is our words that will make or break kingdoms.

Unfortunately, despite all our efforts and measures, our verdict was passed in April 1927. Several of my comrades were given life sentences, some of them in very extreme circumstances in *kalapani,* the cellular jail. I know that this is not going to be easy for them and I send out my blessings, love and strength so that they can carry on with dignity and provide an undying love for the nation.

With a heavy heart, and injured pride I tell you that along with my beloved Ashfaqullah Khan, Rajendra Nath

Lahiri and Thakur Roshan Singh, I had been sentenced to death.

•

When the verdict came out, the country was washed over with a wave of anger and sadness. I know of cries of protests outside the prison and every time we were being transported from one location to another, I could see the desperation in the eyes of those who surrounded us. I even felt the sympathy and anger of the fellow prisoners and even some policemen, who I had grown to understand before and during the course of my imprisonment. I got to know later that a written memorandum was sent to the viceroy and Governor General of India, Lord Irwin through the efforts led by Madan Mohan Malaviya. This memorandum contained the signatures of 78 members of the central legislature and begged for an appeal.

But it was turned down. I am happy to tell you that the support did not stop here. A final appeal of mercy was also sent to the Privy Council at London through Henry SL Pollock, who was a very famous lawyer in England.

But I can imagine how insulting and infuriating it would have been for the British government. After all, a bunch of youngsters had put them to shame. I think even before the trial had begun, their minds had been made up about giving us the ultimate punishment, because they wanted to set a strong precedent and a message not only to the country, but to the world that the British Empire would not be taken lightly.

I doubt whether giving death sentences to youngsters and teenagers would really be a sign of bravado and strength.

I know that the songs of our journey are being sung around the country and are being covered extensively by the media.

Several articles have been written by Bhagat Singh himself in as many newspapers as he could access. The youth were angry like never before and the revolution blazed with a new fire.

14

"ऐ मातृभूमि तेरी जय हो, सदा विजय हो।
प्रत्येक भक्त तेरा, सुख-शान्ति-कान्तिमय हो।"

"Dear motherland, I bow down to you, may you always be victorious. May every follower of yours always be happy, at peace and prosperous."

The appeals are futile and the government is not ready to budge. So many appeals, so many protests and so many petitions have been filed. But alas, there has been no intention of sympathy from the government's side.

But that is alright. I don't expect to bow down in front of these supremacists who have thought of us as nothing less than the dirt under their feet. They thought they would tie us down, beat us and bring us on our knees, while they ride their high horses. They cannot tell us who we are and how we should be living our lives. They think that putting a man behind bars would take away his love for the country or would even stop him from moving forward for the sake of his nation. They forget that we are Indians and it will take a lot more than some iron bars to hold us back. I am writing these letters, as I will continue to write till my last breath, because I know that the nation loves me and is looking at my every action to find direction and motivation.

My words, my thoughts and even my life, are not for myself, but for the youth of the country. I had believed that some of the wise and intelligent British officers I had met were people of honour. The Empire claims in front of the whole world that it's a well-wisher and that they are here for fair rule and governance. Which is why, through my appeals, I had hoped that they would at least try to uphold their image. I only scoff at them now, at their two-faced agenda.

This is not surprising, however, because I know that they had intended this all along. A deadline of 19 December 1927 has been set and the time of execution has been set at 6:30 a.m.

I know that death is near now and I am wondering, looking back in time, about all the actions and consequences that happened. I am thinking about how I have landed up in this situation. I am wondering if it was all worth it.

In the larger scheme of things, this one little robbery, where we all were labelled as dacoits who only came to harm government property, may not look like such a big deal to unknown observers. But there is so much that has happened because of it.

I can see that despite the attempts of all those who did not want the revolutionaries to rise, a wave of emotions has started to grow and there are many people joining in.

I have been testing my faith and my strengths for too long. There were so many instances where I could have simply escaped. Even before and during my arrest, the police have treated me with such carelessness that it would not have taken me a lot of effort to leave. Even when I was picked up from my house, I loitered around the streets for about half an hour unbound, before I gave up my thoughts and decided to go to the police station. All this while, the police patiently stood by and let me do whatever I wanted. I also felt that I needed some space, and in some way, I hope they were all empathising with the cause.

Even when I reached the police station, nobody talked about tying me up. I was left under the charge of a very laid-back policeman and the clerk who was busy finishing his documentation. The rest of the police had left to make other coordinated arrests that were scheduled for the day. The police officer was so careless that I could have left right in front of him and he would not have noticed. The clerk who was working at the desk was a known person to me.

I contemplated even at that time to make the escape and even discussed this with him. But he came down on his knees and begged me not to do it. I knew that his job would be on the line and then there was no telling what would happen to him and his family.

I could not bear to think about the harm that I would cause, simply by trying to make the escape. So I just sat there and waited. Even when the rest of the officers returned, they placed a lot of recovered weapons around me. There were guns and bullets recovered from Ashfaq's brother and were lying right in front of me on the table. I was still not tied up and could easily have picked up a gun. Nobody could have stopped me from escaping.

But again, I thought about the staff and felt responsible for their family and future. The thoughts of escaping the jail kept looming in my mind again and again. I requested to go to the lavatory and one of the policemen suggested tying my hands, but the gentleman who was to escort me believed in my integrity. He said that he knew me well enough to believe that I would not try anything fraudulent.

I went into the lavatory while the policeman went ahead to check out some feud that was going on in the field nearby. I could have easily jumped off the wall and run away before anyone would have even noticed that I was gone. But the moment I thought about what would happen later stopped me from taking such a step. The policeman who had vouched for my character would be blamed and then, his family might also suffer.

•

There were several other occasions of escape, but something or the other always held me back. Our initial days in the Lucknow jail had been very carefree. The officer in charge of the jail at that time was Pandit Champalal ji. He always held us in very high regard and treated us like his own children. We were allowed to roam around freely and had most of our demands and tantrums met with affection. I cannot imagine having been treated better even in my own family.

The policemen were extremely careless around us. The guard, who was in charge of taking care of me, would sleep right in front of my eyes. We had built such a rapport in the jail that nobody really treated us as prisoners. There were so many times when I thought I could simply pull out the iron bars that I had originally cut in my cell and simply escape when the guard was asleep. But my thoughts would always go back to Pandit Champalal ji and the consequences he would have to face. I had suffered a betrayal and it shook me up to imagine how he would feel if I betrayed his trust and love.

Let me clarify that I am not boasting about my selflessness. I was not the only one who felt this way. I guess what I'm trying to help you understand is that when you are on a path for the larger good, when you are thinking about your fellow countrymen and your motherland more than your own life, your thoughts are bound to go just beyond your own interest and turn you into some kind of a philanthropist with integrity that goes beyond your own interests.

It's not even like I really wanted to escape the prison because quite frankly, the state in which the country had been was beginning to pull me down tremendously. There had been so much opposition to the revolutionaries that it was heart-breaking to see how our sacrifices were being treated. The government was trying to defame us in any way possible. The aristocrats and the rich population of the country also treated us with disdain and disapproval.

After all, what kind of gain did they have from the revolution? These were people who were in the good books of the government and enjoyed all the privileges during the British Raj. They were complacent and confident. They did not have to give up on anything and had a considerable amount of say in the administration because of their money and power.

What did they understand about the situation of the farmer who was being exploited to the point of his death?

What did they understand about the lives of those who did not have a single penny to their name and had to go by begging, borrowing or stealing?

The ruling class generally wants to maintain status quo. They are too comfortable and easy to bring about any kind of change. The revolutionaries were nothing more than a disturbance and destruction for them, which is why they tried their best to make us appear destructive or inexperienced, irrational youngsters.

What they did not know or even understand, however, was that it was our hardship and struggle, our scarcity and deprivation that made us strong and resilient to the level of being brazenly confident and determined to move mountains. Who else, without the backing of families, political leaders or even resources would dare to face the Empire and rob a train?! Who else would have the ardent vision to create a disruption to their name and respect being sabotaged by a mere bunch of teenagers? I am not arrogant, dear reader, but I want you to understand that while I do not want to dramatise or romanticise our deprivations, I believe we revolutionaries have been stronger, not despite our struggles but because of them! And we will continue with the war, no matter where we are.

The unfortunate truth is that the war of independence has been going in an erratic and unorganised manner. There is no clear leadership and different schools of thoughts are continuing their own actions with their respective agenda. This is what happens when there is a population which is devoid of education and understanding of the larger concepts of politics. This is what happens when misguided philosophies and personal agenda are added in the form of nationalistic movements and forced on people who otherwise are oblivious to it.

As common people, we become gullible and vulnerable to the propaganda and then go around following movements in spurts of excitement. This is the reason why India did not mobilise its population to a focused and dedicated movement for independence. It does not take a great deal of resources or extraordinary mettle to raise a revolution. World history and politics has shown us people like Lenin and Chhatrapati Shivaji, who have risen from humble beginnings and transformed the course of history because of their intellectual strength and the power of their determination.

I wish more youngsters in this country are able to understand and appreciate the importance of education. I don't mean having degrees, but an in-depth understanding of our world and nuanced perception of different philosophies and concepts of the world.

If we are able to reach that level of intellectualism, we will become an evolved nation with an atmosphere where people are able to deliberate and then, form an informed opinion. I am fortunate enough to have had access to that kind of literature in my life. That is also the reason why I am writing all of this, dear readers!

If through my own humble experiences and insights, I am able to express even an iota of knowledge into my writings, then I am hoping to carry forward this culture of reading and writing over to the next generation. I do not know if my writings will become popular, but if you are able to read this, I hope that my own experiences will at least give you a guiding light which can guide your path forward.

•

I am at the last leg of my life now. I wonder if you can imagine the various emotions that I am feeling right now.

On one hand, there is anger and frustration. After all, I'm only human. When I look back in time, I think about all the things that I could have done differently or should have done differently, not only because I am in prison now and I have a death sentence hanging over my head. But, I also say this because if I had made different decisions, it could have led to different consequences that could have helped me promote the cause for my country and get significant results.

I hope I don't have to prove anymore that my actions and ideals have always been dedicated for my beloved country. If you sense anguish in my voice right now, it is because I want to do more. I want to be alive, not because I love my life, but because I know the youth of the world looks up to me and I know there's a lot to be done.

I do not want the journey to finish only at bringing India to her independence, but to set the way through which our motherland can grow and flourish. I want to see opportunities and fair pathways, education and careers, development and brotherhood, that is not limited to the top layer, but brought down to the backbone of the country. I want to translate our progressive vision into reality, giving rise to a developed nation.

I wish I would have been able to strengthen my organisation and bring people closer together. I also feel the desperation of not having an opportunity to escape now. I wish that the country was looking after the people who are ready to lay their lives for her.

But having said this, I also feel a deep sense of gratitude. I am indebted to this country for making me what I am today and for giving me the opportunity to contribute even in the most insignificant manner. I am proud that I got to rise from being a nobody to being able to lead an organisation. I hope I am able to give some sense of direction to the youth of this country. I also see rays of hope in the way that the communal tone of the country has been changing.

The bond between me and my beloved friend Ashfaqullah Khan is no secret. In fact, the very statement given out by the government has declared that Ashfaqullah Khan and I were primary confidants. We led this operation of the Kakori robbery in cooperation with one another. When the government has been trying to break down our collective efforts towards freedom through any means possible, communal disharmony has become a common practice.

But now, I am happy to say that because of the kind of example we have set through our friendship, people started believing in the strong, unconditional bond that could exist between Hindus and Muslims.

Ashfaq's endless contribution in mobilizing the Muslim community towards the cause of revolution has helped to set a tone of uniting the two communities that had otherwise become distant in the recent past. Now, I see more and more people coming together from both the religions, joining the organisation or even otherwise, working towards the cause of independence. I see several other Muslim bodies joining hands with the Hindu communities.

I won't ever take credit for this entire movement because it was a joint effort made by all of us. I hope that our bond and complete faith in each other has helped set an example that the future of our country holds far more value than the trivial differences of religion that the British Raj has been creating for their own benefit.

In a way, I am also happy that I am away from the dirty politics going on in some parts of the country. For their own vested interests, people have been trying to pull down the reputation of the revolutionaries or even misguide the different movements arising in the country so that their own agendas can be met. I don't know how I would have been able to take this and whether I would have dug a deeper hole for myself and HRA in voicing my own opinions on these matters.

Right now, I stand like a distant witness, unable to make any active contribution for my beloved country. I am hoping that my words will be able to send across at least some kind of message that may come in handy for youngsters somewhere in the country, who are also trying to find their own standing and opinions in a world that is heavily misdirected. This, I believe, is a very unique kind of learning that is helping me understand, from an objective learner's perspective. My mistakes are also inspiring and full of learning. I see now the many benefits of making mistakes because they make me stronger and wiser.

•

Interestingly, this was also a time when I was getting to know more about myself. Growing up, we did not have the luxury of the time to invest in ourselves, considering the kind of deprived background we were coming from. Besides, it is not a common culture in India to really invest in yourself because most of our struggles are anyway focused towards staying alive, being able to earn a living and to gather enough resources to at least have a secured future. In such a scenario, delving deeper into the philosophical and spiritual side of the self is neither common nor easy.

However, I was lucky enough to find good company and direction from a very young age. I was able to meet people and take guidance from gurus who were exceptionally enlightened and blessed me with the knowledge and determination to continue on the right path.

I was lucky to have a mother who made sure that my sisters were not killed at birth and that we were given the right kind of upbringing that was philanthropic, inclusive and ethical. She gave us space to make our own decisions and guide us towards the consequences of those decisions instead of imposing her own opinions on us. I know that my father and my grandmother came from a different school of thought. They tried to impose the traditional and conservative school of thought on me. But my mother was really ahead of her time and she made sure that I would at least get the opportunity to go beyond the narrow horizon of thinking that my paternal family believed in.

Often times, she would protect me from the anger of my father. She would push me towards exploring life and support me in my decisions. I would not say that she spoiled me, but whenever I raised a request for anything, including money, which was hard to get by that time, she never refused. I think it was this blind trust and confidence that she had in me that pushed me towards choosing the better path. She always encouraged me to read and even write. I still don't know how many of her own dreams she must have given up to make sure that I got a chance to follow mine. I don't know how she managed to get that money for me.

I also don't know how she became the progressive person that she was, considering the time that we lived in. She must be a blessed soul who came from another time and in many ways was the root cause for giving me the direction and the confidence to become the person I am.

•

As a staunch follower of Arya Samaj from a very young age, I used to practice yoga. I strictly followed the laws of the Arya Samaji literature. However, growing up with the struggles of depravity and the routine that had me completely immersed in the activities of the organisation, I did not have the time or the energy to pursue my sincere interest of spiritual understanding of the self. I followed the physical routine like waking up in the morning and sincerely pursued my prayer routine. But it was a lot less than what I would have really liked to do.

It is true that the discovery of the soul can only be followed when the basic needs of life have been met. Only those who do not have to struggle for food and shelter every day can really be carefree enough to shut out the external world and dive deeper into themselves. Ironically though, I do not see a lot of rich and affluent going on the path of spiritual discovery, because they are still trapped in the nourishment of the wealth of the world.

On the other hand, the position that I have been in over the last few months has been a blessing in disguise. It has helped me give up my worldly engagements. My food and shelter, as understated as it can be, is at least something that I don't have to worry about.

My cell is minimalistic and even takes away the opportunity of a shaded tree in the scorching heat. You can imagine that I have nothing to lose here. I have taken this as an opportunity to refocus my thoughts on my spiritual journey. I always wanted to live my life as a sage or an ascetic. I wanted to practice higher levels of yoga and wanted to give up the needs of the body and feed the fire of the soul. I am happy to write that my time in prison has given me the opportunity to do this.

•

Even when I was in the prison in Lucknow, I got a chance to practice my principles of Arya Samaj. I would wake up in the morning and conduct the hawan. I would pray and talk about true knowledge. In fact, even in that prison there were so many people who had started treating me like some sort of a guru or saint. They would come to me to listen to my conversations and sometimes even ask for my blessings if there was a problem going on in their lives. I don't know whether my blessings helped them or not, but I do know that it gave me an opportunity to look forward to deeper understanding and spiritual growth.

Now the only things that keep me engaged are these pages full of expressions of my thoughts and experiences, and my practice of yoga and *sadhana*[14]. It is unfortunate that this growth and discovery won't have any significant consequences in my life now, which is about to end in a few days. But I hope that the writings will help me to express to myself and to the world about things that really matter.

I am wondering if there is a lesson in this for all of us to follow a path of minimalism and to never lose priority over what really matters in the bigger picture, about what is really under our control and what is the path that we truly need to adopt in our lives. It is not out of jealousy or spite that I say this, but I wonder if all the luxury in the world, all the kingdoms and the land would ever help people think about these things and to guide themselves in such a direction.

All the great men and women who I have read about, who found their own calling and were able to pursue their dreams with the degree of strength and courage, were people who came from minimalistic backgrounds. Even those who

---

14. Meditation

came from a life of luxury had to give up their comfort and privileges in order to pursue their true calling. Gautam Buddha only found his enlightenment when he gave up all that was engaging him and trapping him in worldly affairs.

Nowhere comparing myself to these heroes, at least I am able to recognise the process and the direction that such an opportunity can bring into our lives.

•

My execution was pushed beyond the reasonable time, and I know this was done so I could suffer in this prison all through the scorching heat of the summer. They deliberately chose this location where I would not even have a shaded tree to cool down the bricks of these walls in the peak of the summer season. They made sure that I barely had a blanket to use, or a cushion to sleep at night. I think their intention was to punish me to such a level that I would start regretting my actions. On the contrary, they have helped me delve deeper into my own thought process. They have helped me refocus my energy and remaining time of my life towards strengthening my own philosophies, rediscovering my insights and, above all, being able to pen down my thoughts, even under these circumstances.

It is possible that if I had a more luxurious setup or if I was in a more comfortable position, I would have been tempted to take my thoughts into other directions. I may have been more desperate to escape or to think about what could have been. I am able to write this with contentment because deprivations bring you just as much accomplishment, if you manage to rise above your needs. This, I believe, is a very unique kind of learning that is helping me understand from an objective learner's perspective.

My mistakes are also inspiring. I see now the many benefits of making mistakes because they make me stronger and wiser.

These are probably my last words to you, dear reader.

•

I want to admit that although the loss of my life is something that makes me nervous, I am not afraid anymore. I know that I could not have asked for a better way to give my life to my country. I send out my love and blessings to all of my comrades who have just as selflessly and briefly given up their lives and put blind faith in me.

I have no regrets whatsoever. I did try to make applications to the privy council to delay the execution, because honestly, I am curious to understand what happens to the organisation and to see the course the country takes towards independence. The government has not budged and I know that this will definitely be the last of my opportunities. I urge you all to educate yourself and one another, not only through schools and colleges, but also to open your minds towards the different perspectives that can harmoniously coexist.

I strongly urge you to continuously work towards looking for a calling and no matter what philosophy you follow or what school of thought you adopt, remember that there is always scope for growth. The only thing I would strongly urge you to do is to look out for more people and to work collectively and in cooperation with one another towards the cause of the nation because that is the very principle that will defeat the intentions of the British who have been trying to break us down into little bits and pieces.

If we are able to be resilient towards this one weakness and are able to overcome our differences, then there is no stopping us. With a collective population with the abundance of our culture and resources, we can become the strongest army in the world and no external force will ever be able to break us down.

And yet, if we take our weaknesses to heart and make them the foundation of our beliefs, then we will not need any external force to break us. We will make ourselves hollow from inside. I hope the nation sees freedom soon and my dreams are fulfilled.

> "I tried to make India free and the attempt will not end with my life."
>
> – Ram Prasad Bismil
>
> *(The Revolutionary - Translation of the Autobiography of Ram Prasad Bismil – Meri Atmakatha)*

Epilogue

"अगर आपके लहू में रोष नहीं है, तो ये पानी है जो आपकी रगो में बह रहा है।"

"If your blood does not rage, it is water that flows in your veins."

My dear friend, have you heard of this little town called Kakori in northern India?

An easy visit to the small town of Kakori, a mere sixteen kilometres from Lucknow in Uttar Pradesh, can bring you to the legendary epicentre which was the first and the most significant organised attack on the British Raj. What happened here set into motion the events that resulted in a big change for the country.

Most people don't know that I have hidden for many years, observing the fate of a country for which many people have given their lives, let go of livelihoods that have affected generations of their family – all for the love of the motherland.

I am also writing about all this because I have seen the narrative of independence change. I want to make sure that at least this account lives to tell the tale of the brave men and what remains of the country afterwards.

My name is Chandra Shekhar, commonly known as Azad, because that is my dream for the country and our spirits. I am expressing my thoughts with a heavy heart, because the one person who should really have seen the dawn of a free India is no more with us. It is my duty and honour to express my gratitude to his undying spirit on behalf of all the brothers and sisters whose life Bismil has inspired.

Dear reader, you will hear many different versions of this struggle of independence. However, history is told from different perspectives and it requires a deep uncovering to understand the strengths and struggles of the heroes of the Kakori action, the first step towards the war of independence.

Towards the end of his life, Bismil – imprisoned in the small, inhumane captivity of a small jail in Gorakhpur – talked about his emotions in an authentic manner. His words explained the pain and frustration of the very humanised, non-glorified days of the hero who had set in motion what is considered the first most explosive and impactful movement of revolution for the Indian war of independence, since the revolt of 1857.

I personally looked up to him and had the good fortune of carrying forward his legacy by rebuilding his beloved organisation when it was falling apart from the misery of his death. I also had the privilege of meeting him through the Bengali *tola* of freedom fighters in Banaras. I am proud to say that we became confidants really soon. I was with him during the Kakori operation and got to know him well.

I am not sure whether to count myself lucky or unfortunate that I escaped the arrest for the Kakori robbery. I cannot describe my angst and frustration at being a bystander when my comrades were struggling in prisons, alone and in misery.

I tried desperately, but failed to rescue them. Bhagat Singh and I had made several attempts, with whatever little resources we had in hand, but we could not rescue Bismil.

His death sentence had felt like a bullet right through my chest and yet, towards the end of his life, I could not even manage to take a gun to his cell so this man could at least get a fair chance to escape his unjust death with untiring strength.

Initially, we would try to keep a track on where his movements were going to be and what developments were happening in his case. We also tried to reach out to him about the development which involved other people. We tried to give him updates about the organisation, about the other political movements happening around the country and as much intelligence as we could find on the other prisoners of the Kakori robbery.

This was not easy, because I was on the run and had to stay hidden. On the other hand, it pains me to say that the information that we were able to pass on to him was also not pleasant and comforting. The country had been going into shambles. The few elite political leaders were trying their best to make sure that the Hindustan Republican Association would collapse. This was achieved by fabricating stories of how a bunch of youngsters failed in their poorly executed operations.

I revere the political leaders who have taken the throne on behalf of India and represent us in the country's journey towards progress. But just as Bismil did, I also hold my reservations against those who have misunderstood him and spread misinformation about him and his agenda. They have clearly done this for meeting their own political ends, and regaining lost power and control.

After all, it is not easy for the experienced leaders, who have earned so much fame and popularity among the masses, to be told publicly that they have disappointed the youth of the country. Not a lot of people have had the courage to come out in the open and oppose the well-established stalwarts of the political struggle of the country.

But young Bismil, filled with passion and dedication, had the courage to go up to Gandhi and speak his mind out in the Congress convention.

Bismil had grown up being inspired by Gandhi's philosophies of non-cooperation and non-violence. Being the academically oriented disciplinarian that he was, he tried his best to follow any literature that was available to expand on these schools of thought.

He had been deeply inspired by the non-cooperation movement. And this man had single-handedly mobilised many youngsters, both men and women, to join the non-cooperation movement. He saw a significant contribution that this could make in the longer run. You can imagine how heartbroken he must have been when the non-cooperation movement was called off. He felt betrayed and dejected.

But unlike most people in the country, who believe in staying in the good books and doing what is convenient in the name of politics, this man was never the one to be scared or to mince his words to be politically and socially appropriate. He had reprimanded Gandhi in front of the entire conference's participants and expressed his point of view boldly and smartly.

I am not talking about an influential senior leader who has earned the authority to take up the floor and express his views so vehemently. I am talking about a youngster, who came from humble beginnings, who had taught himself to build a solid understanding of the philosophies and politics of the world. But he spoke with such passion that its impact will remain unmatched even for the most seasoned orators and public speakers of our times.

When Bismil was jailed, most of us did not take this as the final verdict and strongly believed that we would be able to rescue him from behind the bars and continue the movement with an even stronger commitment. Not for once did we imagine the future of the Hindustan Republican Association without its founder.

We tried our best to coordinate and arrange for resources and information that would help in rescuing Bismil and others. In most of these endeavours, Bhagat Singh was one of the most prominent figures, who were just as passionately and sincerely involved in trying to help with the rescue plans.

We tried to trace the route between the court and the police station in Lucknow more than once. We tried to understand where the transfer happened and where he was placed in the prison so that we could rescue him on the way back from the court at a time where most of the guards were occupied in the proceedings of the trial and did not pay close attention to the security. However, there must have been something that we did wrong or some judgment that went awry from our side.

Was it that there was perhaps a mole amongst us? Or some carelessness because of which we had leaked the information of our plan out in the open? Because suddenly, the transfer of Bismil and the others from the court to the prison became a very prominent event with a lot many additional forces applied for the sake of security and backup.

We were right there, strategically hidden in the crowd, so that no one could identify us. And yet, we could not manage to rescue him because of all these extra people and policemen who had been put on guard.

We were just a handful of revolutionaries with barely any weapons and it was wise to admit defeat rather than risking our own lives and lives of the other comrades in the process.

•

There was this one time when I had the opportunity to rescue him when he was being transferred between Kanpur and Lucknow. Bhagat Singh and I, along with a couple of other colleagues had built up a plan which would simply require following the route and sneaking Bismil out of captivity. We could have managed this because we understood the route and we also understood the capacities of the policemen who were holding him captive. We had scanned that area several times and had anticipated all the things that could go wrong. However, it felt even fate was against us at that time.

At the Kanpur railway station, on the day where we arrived to follow their entourage, when we were in the process of buying tickets to reach Lucknow. I reached out for my wallet to find that it had been stolen. The wallet contained whatever little money we had that was crucial for this rescue operation.

It also contained my driving licence and a few other important notes. We lost all of that. Nobody else had money. Out of all the things that could have happened, this was extremely unfortunate and ridiculous. It felt like destiny was also laughing at us, by stopping us with something as petty as a theft.

Of course, I was shocked and kicked myself endlessly. How could I let something like this happen on such an important day? We did not have any money to carry out the plan and for something as small as that, the rescue mission for our beloved Bismil was cancelled.

I tried to keep myself strong and looked into the future, thinking that we would definitely get more opportunities to do this. Taking this with a pinch of salt, as a lesson for myself that while my eyes were on the bigger picture, I should not have lost sight of my footing on the ground.

However, I saw Bhagat Singh breakdown into tears, sobbing like a child. Although he had never really worked very closely with Bismil, the young revolutionary was deeply inspired by Bismil's life and his initiatives for the country.

•

Bhagat Singh had written several times in the media about the Kakori robbery. He had also infamously written character sketches of the participants of the Kakori robbery, praising them like heroes and setting example for the country, especially for the youth to understand who these people were, what their objectives were and why they were behind bars. He understood that we were following our passion and love for the country and trying to set into motion a revolution that the entire nation would follow. It has been awe-inspiring for me to see not only Bhagat Singh but so many youngsters who have been inspired and guided by the words of Bismil.

In a true sense, he has been a revolutionary who not only formed the course of the country's struggle for independence, but also changed the tone and modality through which we were expecting a message. It is because of him that so many youngsters were oriented towards reading and writing rich and important literature of the world. It was also because of him that the youngsters found a purpose and direction.

•

Dear reader, I hope that the future of free India has been kind to its heroes and told you the tales of how men like Bismil rose to become immortals in the eyes of the nation. But I also hope you get to hear the harsh truth about the darker side of the moon, which is often omitted from our stories. Towards the end of his days, right up to the point when Bismil was hung to death, let alone being given the respect of being treated like a political prisoner, he was left isolated by most of the people who he had counted on.

While the country was storming with the heroic trumpets of mass revolts, publications and marches being led by the popular wings of the revolution, a small group of people were still struggling to bring the educated and informed youth of the country into a streamlined and organised march towards independence. We were trying to restore the pillars of revolution that Bismil and his comrades had established.

The Kakori Robbery had done many things and if its impact was to be broken down, there would be buckets of categories including financial impact, social pressure, legal implications, political realignment of leaders, as well as a philosophical shift in the uprising.

I think you may have understood Bismil's desperate insistence to prove that the youth of the country was worth relying on. That contrary to popular belief, we are a group of intelligent, educated and ethically sound men and women, even though we have been defamed as being impulsive, violent, short-sighted and more. Up until the Kakori incident, thefts and robberies had been seen as petty crimes and acts of violence, not just by the Raj or the masses but even by the more right winged leaders who were struggling for independence.

Bismil, despite his disappointment with Gandhi, had been a strong promoter of the non-cooperation movement and despite his difference of opinion with Bapu, held high regards for his principles and passion for the country. I have vivid memories of his vehemence against conducting robberies against Indians –which, albeit were acted out of the drive to collect money for the movement, for arranging for travel, literature, publications, mobilisations and of course weaponry –was unfortunately leading to violence against fellow Indians and unintentionally also leading to shoot-outs, injuries, and even death.

More than anything else, my brave and wise friend was extremely mindful towards the example we were setting for others to follow. This led to his personal and collective decisions of putting a stop to such attacks that were, in the core, causing losses to Indians. There was general categorisation of historians, politicians and media of war heroes of independence into very black and white boundaries of right winged congressmen or extremists, pro-violence or non-violence and pro-Partition or integration. But as someone who has been witnessing the different sects and generations of revolutionaries, I would like to insist that in principle, we were connected to the same cause of independence. We held respect, understanding and acceptance for each other and were headed, albeit through different roads, towards the same destination. Bismil's idea of going as far as possible with non-violence was heavily inspired by Gandhi's principles and in-turn, led for the aggressive youth across the country to channel their energy into sound actions.

As someone who got to witness the foundation of the Hindustan Republican Association, and to lead its reconstruction after Bismil's death, I can confidently speak of my observations of the connections and inspirations that were transmitted through generations of freedom fighters. Bismil was a representative of the very educated, informed and passionate youth that was inspired and connected with world politics and philosophy and found themselves drawn from the leaders around the world.

•

The legacy created by the brave men like Bismil and Ashfaqullah was transferred to the younger generation of people like Bhagat Singh. Although Bhagat Singh had not been directly involved in the Kakori robbery, the strength in the movement started by HRA inspired him deeply to travel from Punjab to Kanpur to meet the leaders who were already driving the youth across the country. His influence is strongly reflected in the character sketches he wrote about those who had played key roles in the Kakori action. He narrated this extensively in the Punjabi newsletter, *Keerti,* for which he was also arrested. In fact, we had together made many attempts to support the Kakori revolutionaries and to rescue them from prison.

I cannot explain how my heart cries reading Bismil's desperate calls for rescue, in the form of ghazals and letters, beckoning his fellow freedom fighters to help their escape in any way possible, after the death sentence had been passed. Bhagat Singh personally came to Lucknow twice to concoct a rescue operation, which was however hampered due to information leak to the police guards. That resulted in increase in security in both attempts.

Contrary to the common image of Bhagat Singh of being the brave-heart, tall, masculine figure, I myself have witnessed the very vulnerable side of him. I remember Bhagat Singh breaking down at not being able to rescue Bismil or even Jogesh Chandra Chatterjee due to stupid mistakes or unavoidable mishaps. His passion as a teenager and his dedication towards following his predecessors reveals his delicate side just as much as his heroism.

Despite being pitched as someone who opposed the Gandhian philosophy of non-violence, Bhagat Singh himself, deeply inspired by the actions of Bismil and Ashfaq in prison, went on a hunger strike in protest, thus marking his association with the same principles. Several such episodes have revealed the resemblance and amalgamation of philosophies of different schools amidst leaders who are today portrayed as opposites.

The reason I tell you about all this is so that you understand and realise that our thoughts and beliefs were not all that polarised and as much as the British did try to divide us, we were not all that different in our paths.

-: *Prachi Garg* :-

•

By now, as the nation is deeply soaked in the spirit of revolution, it is clear that the Kakori episode triggered a dynamic plan of revolution amongst the youth. Despite the belief and sentiments spread in current records and propaganda, the belief systems of the Congress and the HRA were not all that different. In fact, despite their difference of opinion, my comrades and friends, who had been arrested after the Kakori action, had all turned to hunger strike in protest to being treated like ordinary prisoners without the typical privileges assigned to political prisoners.

I want to remind you that for the sake of convenience and politics, often times, such similarities and inspirations are ignored in the benefit of projections of different schools of politics. But as someone who has witnessed these movements first-hand and watched principles and courses melt from one form to another, I can tell you that at the root, we have all been the same.

In fact, the death sentence of Bismil, Lahiri, Ashfaq and Roshan Singh was also responsible in a way for bringing leaders across sects together to work against the verdict passed for the Kakori-event revolutionaries, including prominent leaders like Motilal Nehru.

It was this legacy that continued in the form of reconstruction of the HRA into the HSRA - Hindustan

Socialist Republican Association, and I played a humble role of leading this reconstitution.

The vision was not only to continue the struggle of independence, but also visualising how the post-independence scenario of the country would look like. We did this by adding the word socialist into the name, as well as adding sections to its manifesto, narrating the vision of a socialist, republican nation. It was also this wing of the revolution that brought about strong, educated youth into the movement, with dedicated steps towards creating publications, books, memoirs, campaigns and other forms of literature.

This fresh wave brought with it the knowledge of inspirational movements from across the world and the nation to the rising masses, thereby creating a refined, politically and philosophically awakened school of freedom fighters. They were headed towards not just taking India to its independence, but also looking futuristically into building the formative generation for constituting the free nation.

I would like to believe that the HSRA is a continuation of the dream that Bismil had for all of us. I humbly wish to carry on with his philosophies, inspiring the youth and guiding them in a direction that gives them strength and wisdom to dedicate their lives for the motherland.

The popularity of the pivotal Kakori event gave birth to literature of different genres, which, despite its misrepresentation, still bears witness to the holistic and often intersecting movements for independence. I am sure you understand why, despite tears in my eyes and guns chasing me, I still feel the responsibility to contribute to these narratives that may help the future generations understand our sentiments.

This afterthought of the Kakori action would be incomplete without a reflection on the final days of the heroes of the struggle, who were, unfortunately reduced to a state of abandonment. Bismil penned down his experiences so that the youth can take inspiration from his journey, despite his misery. While showcasing the entire path of struggle, he also honestly depicted the failures of the nation in rescuing its heroes at their worst and most vulnerable positions. His letters, his poems and songs that reached us from that prison in Gorakhpur recounted the situation of his jail. They are a gruesome reflection of dejection and reveal a far deeper truth that the nation's population was perhaps not as willing to take risks for the freedom fighters.

•

Bismil's last days, spent in a prison cell, with barely any ventilation or anything more than a couple of blankets in the name of comfort, makes me shudder. Bismil led the movement that brought singularly the most triggering impact on what became a full-fledged war of independence. He expressed no remorse in being imprisoned or being sentenced to death, but

I know very well that we had disappointed him and failed him as a friend, a comrade and a hero who deserved a lot more support.

All the words and thoughts that Bismil shared with us are not far from the truth as there were many other heroes who spent their last days in isolation and dejection. Though worshipped for their bravery, they were still reduced to being far less than heroes in their last days, waiting for the help that did not arrive. Nothing could extinguish their fire of the courageous men whose bodies were locked but the spirits could not be tamed or controlled by the chains of the empire.

While the country has its own version of the stories, the whole truth is lost between the pages where generations of freedom fighters, despite their differences had struggled, sacrificed and succeeded together. I know that decades from now, even this version of history may be forgotten or distorted. But I hope that my words will help you take a closer look at the truth so that understand the purpose and reality of our struggles.

Now that we are a step closer to attaining our freedom, I am poised to take up the reins and move on with vigour and passion. With Bismil's blessings, I strive to fight with all my might, taking the battle forward to its glorious end.

References

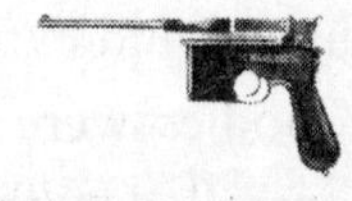

1. Bismil, Ram Pratap. *Atmakatha*. Sahityashil Prakashan, 2012.
2. Singh, Bhagat. *Jail Diary and Other Writings*. New Delhi: General Press, 2020
3. Singh, Bhagat. *Why I am an Atheist and Other Works*. New Delhi: Srishti Publishers, 2019.
4. https://www.britannica.com/topic/Kakori-Conspiracy
5. https://blog.savaari.com/kakori-train-robbery/
6. https://www.youtube.com/watch?v=p3txH75FRTs
7. https://www.youtube.com/watch?v=K3WxC-GNe44
8. https://www.thelallantop.com/bherant/the-story-of-kakori-train-heist-and-creation-of-hindustan-republican-association/
9. https://www.firstpost.com/living/revolutionary-road-a-new-in-depth-look-at-ideology-of-bhagat-singh-azad-2707898.html
10. https://news.cornell.edu/stories/2018/01/historian-examines-

indias-gentlemen-terrorists

11. https://www.opindia.com/2020/08/kakori-train-robbery-indian-independence/
12. https://www.amazon.com.au/AZAD-INVINCIBLE-Babu-Krishnamurthy/dp/B09QJZ3S3P/
13. https://byjus.com/free-ias-prep/kakori-conspiracy/

By the same author

Superwomen
SuperSiblings
SuperCouples
The Legends of a Startup Guy
Startup Secrets from the Ramayana
Ganesha's Global Startup